Cursed
A Novel of The Chosen

Ann Mayburn

Cursed

A Novel of The Chosen

Copyright © 2013 Ann Mayburn

Published by Fated Desires Publishing
All rights reserved.
ISBN-13: 978-1-62322-073-0

This book is a work of fiction. The names, characters, places, and incidents are products of the author's imagination or have been used fictitiously and are not to be construed as real. Any resemblance to persons, living or dead, actual events, locals or organizations is entirely coincidental. All rights reserved. With the exception of quotes used in reviews, this book may not be reproduced or used in whole or in part by any means existing without written permission from the author.

Cover Art by Scott Carpenter
Formatted by IRONHORSE Formatting

Blurb

This story was previously published under the title 'Dance of the Gods' and has been extensively revised and updated.

Locked in a demonic curse, Carmella Ramirez has lost the will to love. Once she was the star of the Ramirez Samba School and lived a charmed life. Now, thanks to an old enemy's thirst for revenge, she's the school's reclusive seamstress and living in the dangerous ghetto of Rio de Janeiro. But that's the least of her problems. When the sun sets, a succubus overtakes Carmella's body and uses her beauty to lure men to their death. As the corpses pile up, those controlling Carmella plan to sacrifice her to their demonic god and blame her for the killings.

Her only hope is Sean Kalmus—a world famous musician and warrior of the Celtic god of Music, Maponus. While in Brazil to work the Carnival, Sam's orders by Maponus to find and rescue Carmella turn into something more than they ever could have imagined when Carmella captures Sean's heart.

With Sean's help, Carmella will have to call on her strength, his magic and their love to break herself free before she becomes known as Brazil's most notorious serial killer.

Some say that the age of chivalry is past, that the spirit of romance is dead. The age of chivalry is never past, so long as there is a wrong left unredressed on earth.
—Charles Kingsley

Chapter One

Carmella Ramirez ran a hand over her crimson silk-covered curves and smiled enticingly at the man following her down the alley in the dirty heat of Rio de Janeiro. Her innocent soul slept, blissfully unaware of the murder her body was about to commit. Sure the sinner would follow her, she walked faster down the alley with a little wiggle in her step.

"Hold on, baby." The portly American tourist wiped the sweat streaming down his face out of his eyes with a red handkerchief. "You gotta give me a chance to catch up to that fine Brazilian ass of yours."

The succubus using Carmella's body paused and spun on her six-inch black stiletto heel without even the slightest sway of the icepick-thin point. A woman would have been immediately suspicious of anyone who could skip without a wince down a dark alley in her shoes. She could easily read the tourist's mind, and he thought her ability to walk down the cobblestone alley in heels high enough to give a hooker a nose bleed was merely a reflection of the sensuality that seemed to hang about the stunning brunette like a cloud of expensive perfume.

Dropping her voice to a soft purr, she gave him a smile that sent a tasty wave of lust her way. "It's just a little farther." She stalked over to him and ran her slim, bronze fingers through his thinning hair. Pressing her hips against his, she gave a thrusting gyration that made him gasp. With a soft breath, she murmured, "I can't wait to show you this club. It is going to blow your mind."

He panted against her then popped a mint-scented antacid into his mouth. "I'm not so sure about this. I don't even speak Mexican."

The succubus tried to keep from rolling her eyes. He had to come of his own free will, but that didn't mean she couldn't stack the odds in her favor. "Don't worry. I'll take good care of you." She searched the man's mind for his hidden desires and found the right words to say in order to get him to follow her. "I've never told anyone this..." She traced the man's lips with the fingertips of the stolen mortal body. "But I've always wanted to dress up like a pirate and be punished for my wicked deeds. If you come to the club with me, we could play with their toys. Floggers, canes, maybe a strap to make my ass burn before you fuck me."

The pulse in his temple throbbed in a rapid beat, and the succubus hoped he didn't keel over right here. His soul was exactly what they needed tonight. Young and newly married, this pitiful man repeatedly defiled his sacred covenant to his wife with whores during his business trips.

"Have you..." The man licked his lips and groped her ass like a pillow in need of fluffing. "Have you been a naughty girl?"

He went to kiss her, tongue first, and she spun away from him with a giggle. "Let's hurry. I don't want all the equipment to be gone by the time we get there."

Heels clicking against the cobble stones, she moved deeper into the alley and stopped below a small white neon sign depicting two dice hanging over a black-painted door. A couple enormous garbage bins piled with boxes blocked the view to the street. His hands found her ass again as she knocked an elaborate rhythm on the door. The magical warding on the entrance repulsed her, but the lust and passion it protected made her want to tear the steel down with her bare hands. She could shred the metal as easily as soft cheese if it wasn't for the wards embedded into the building. Fucking magicians were always spoiling her fun.

The heavy, black metal door swung open, and desire poured out in visible waves that the succubus bathed in with a shudder. To her lust was a cool, delicious drink of power that she craved. She ignored the muffled scream of the man next to her as two brawny men wearing leather masks grabbed him and forced him into the bar. One of them immediately broke the man's right ring finger while the other cut his earlobe off, making the man squeal like a pig.

The warmth of pain and pleasure made her sigh, and she held her hands out to the doorway, absorbing the lust coming from the busy interior. She wanted to wallow in the orgy covering the floor of the bar. She wanted to throw this body to the pleasure of anyone who would have it, to drink in the lust, to suck every human inside dry of their passion. It would be enough to sustain her for months and give her the power she required to escape her summoner.

Anger at being denied what she needed by mere humans pushed aside what little reason the succubus had been born with. She was a creature of pure hunger and need, and being denied the feast before her drove her mad with rage. Starvation made her ravenous to fill the never ending void in her damned soul and she fought the bindings securing her to the magician's will.

She began to chant in a foul language damned by the gods of Creation, the words falling from her lips like drops of poison rain. The bouncer yelled in panic over his shoulder, sweat springing out on his brow and rolling down his sunken cheeks. A tall man with dark hair and scars covering his hands pushed a blonde with the body of a porn star off his lap. Against the back wall, the fat American continued to beg and scream as he was shackled and hoisted to dangle from the ceiling. Anticipation shuddered through the succubus as a priest of the demonic god, Guaricana, selected a black leather whip with razor blades at the tip.

The tall man shouted something, grabbing his black cane from the top of the glass and metal bar, and sprinted to stand next to the bouncer as the warding shuddered beneath the succubus's curse.

"I command you to stop," he growled out and held the succubus's gaze. An angry hiss like a hive of bees swarmed from her slender throat. The bouncer quivered in fear, but the tall man looked bored, despite the slight tremble to his hands. He was her summoner, and as such, his word bound her as long as she accepted the body he offered. A sneer lifted his lip. "The sun will be up soon. You must return the body to her bed."

She fought against the power of his command. "Please, just let me inside for a moment. I'll be good." The distress in her voice was real. To be denied that much lust was painful for a succubus, akin to denying a heroin addict a mixing bowl full of the drug.

The man narrowed his eyes. "Do you think I believe for a second that you won't fuck everything that touches you?"

The succubus walked backward, fighting his order every step of the way. "I *need*!" She tried to explain and held her hands out in a pleading gesture as she begged him to understand the unrelenting hunger.

"And I need you in that body." He began to shut the door in her face then paused and studied her. "Listen to me well, succubus. I forbid you from taking any sexual release with this body. I forbid you from doing anything that would endanger the virginity of your stolen form. You will return your host to her apartment, and then you will depart the earth immediately until I summon you again. Do you understand my orders?"

"Yes."

He sneered at her and she wanted to rip his lips off and make him eat them. "Yes, what?"

"Yes, Master," she whispered and turned without another word.

Once out of sight, she fisted her hands and allowed the command to carry her back to the limo waiting to take this body back to its ghetto apartment. Her summoner would eventually slip up, and when he did, she would beg her true master, Guaricana, to let her be the one to devour his soul.

****

Sean Kalmus yawned while he scrolled through his email, stopping when he saw a message from his patron god, Maponus. The Celtic god of Music preferred modern technology for contacting his worshipers, and Sean appreciated that. Nothing like a magical bird singing a message to you to put a kink in your day while you waited in line at the grocery store. He took a gulp of his now cold coffee and gave himself a mental shake.

Coordinating and packing for the trip to Rio had kept him up all night, leaving him mentally and physically drained. Certainly not in the best frame of mind for dealing with his god. With a sigh, he looked out the window of his home in Ireland, wondering if he could sneak a nap in before answering the email. Faint traces of dawn sent runners of pink over the dark ocean beyond the bay windows of his study, reminding him that a new day had already begun and his chance for rest had passed.

If he didn't read the email right away Maponus had been known to send singing chinchilla telegrams while Sean was trying to have an intimate moment with a pretty girl. His patron god had a weird sense of humor, one of the reasons why they got along so well.

Running his hand through his dark auburn hair hard enough to pull out a few strands, he clicked the email and began to read.

My Chosen,
I have work for you while you're in Brazil. There is a young woman in need of rescue, though she does not know it. You will be in a unique position to help her. She's the first flower of spring, hidden by the snow. Be careful. A High Priest of Guaricana has been using her as his stalking-horse.
Maponus

After reading the letter twice, Sean did a search on the Internet for Guaricana. *A Brazilian devil who is worshiped by whipping young men until the blood flows.*

He spun his chair around to face an empty room and threw his hands in the air. "Awesome. Just fucking fantastic. Not only do I have to DJ for the Carnival parade this year, I also get to lock horns with a devil fond of S&M."

With a sigh, he picked up the phone and called Kell, his best friend and crew chief.

"Hello, Sean," Kell said in a raspy voice. "There had better be a good reason you're calling me only...fifteen minutes after I've finally gotten to bed."

"I'm sorry, but I got a little love note from Maponus."

A light clicking on and sheets rustling came over the phone line. "What does Maponus want?" Kell asked, sounding a lot more awake now.

Leaning back into his dark leather chair, Sean looked out the window to watch the dawn breaking over the Celtic Sea. It was a beautiful sight, the meeting of land and water, but he barely saw it. Instead, his sleep-deprived mind was trying to figure out Maponus' message. He pushed himself out of the comfortable chair and walked over to the wide bay window, gazing into the dawn tinting the dark sky with purple and gray light.

Sean's gaze followed the roll of the ocean beyond his cottage. "Well, besides bringing over a crew of fifteen musicians and dancers, coordinating with twenty-four samba clubs, doing a charity DJ event, trying to make the locals understand our heavily accented English—"

"Don't forget romancing a few of those delicious Brazilian lasses." He chuckled then made a harsh grunt. In the background, Sean could hear Mary, Kell's wife, giving him an earful of what would happen to him if he so much as bumped into one of those women.

"Tell Mary I'll keep you out of trouble." Sean laughed. "So, in addition to all that, I also have to find a woman who is 'the first flower of spring' and save her from some Brazilian destruction god who likes to whip young men until the blood flows."

"First flower of spring. Sounds like Maponus' usual vague description. Doesn't seem too bad, except for the demon with a whip part." Kell sighed tiredly. "Well, my friend, I suggest you get some sleep. Regardless of what our god has in store for you, we still have a twelve-hour flight from Dublin to Rio this afternoon."

"I know, I know. Thank you, Kell. Give Mary a kiss for me."

Sean tossed the phone onto his computer chair then strode over to the floor-to-ceiling dark walnut shelves that dominated the north wall. It was filled with all kinds of books, from dog-eared paperbacks to enormous leather-bound volumes. Reaching up, he pulled down a four-foot black metal case from the top shelf with a soft grunt. After setting it down on a small table next to his reading chair, he briefly ran his fingertips over the scrollwork on the case, memories of wielding this sword countless times spilling through his head in a riot of blood and screams. Whistling a complicated tune, he removed the protection spell from around the case and flipped it open.

Inside, a long and beautifully crafted sword shone on its bed of dark green velvet. A simple silver ring pommel adorned the blade, and the guard was a sinuous curve of gleaming metal. The sword itself was long and razor-sharp, with runes and music notes etched into its length. It was a work of art by one of the greatest bladesmiths that Ireland had ever produced, handed down through six generations of Maponus' Chosen and, by some twist of fate, ending up in his care.

Sean stood there for a long time, memories of haphazardly swinging this sword as a green youth playing out in his mind. How eager he had been when the Celtic god of Music had picked him as his Chosen Hand on Earth. Maponus had gifted Sean with the ability to enhance his music into magic. Sean could bring joy to any heart with a simple melody or heal a wounded body and spirit with a song. He could also break bones, rend flesh, and destroy souls with his music, but he preferred to use it for positive actions.

What he wasn't prepared for were the responsibilities that came with such power. At first, all he'd wanted to do was become a famous musician, have an endless supply of willing women, and travel the world using his god's gift. Instead, he'd found himself drawn into dangerous battles with the Forces of Destruction and protecting the innocent. Oh, the fame and women had come, and the world travel, but his greatest satisfaction came from his secret work as a chosen warrior of the gods of Creation.

Stripping off his shirt, he ran his hands over the large and intricate tattoo covering his muscled back, a series of Celtic knots that looked, at first, like a random design. Magic tingled against his palms as he rubbed a lump tightening up his left shoulder and the tense muscle slowly eased beneath his fingertips. Unlike regular tattoos, the intricate design on his back was slightly raised so it felt more like a carving etched into his skin than simply ink beneath the surface. At first the pattern appeared to be nothing more than a massive, intricate series of Celtic knots and magical symbols. It was only after following the path of the twisting lines, and looking at the bigger picture, that it became apparent the design was a series of music notes. The markings had appeared after he completed the full transition from mortal to Chosen, a warning to his enemies that he was under the protection of a powerful god.

Sean took the sword out of its bed of green velvet and held it before him, turning the blade in the dim morning light. Well cared for, the fine edge could cut through metal and bone like warm butter. Every time he put the sword back into its case and on the shelf, he hoped that maybe that would be the last time he would need to wield it, that just maybe he'd earned the right to a moment of peace in his life, a time when he wouldn't be responsible for saving the world and could instead focus on finding a woman strong enough to survive being the beloved of a Chosen. He was so tired of being alone.

Chapter Two

Carmella soaked her sore fingers in a mixing bowl filled with iced water. It would have been nice if she could have gone to the voodoo priestess down the street for a healing balm, but she barely had enough money to pay this month's rent. Oh, she could have gone to a black magic practitioner who would have charged her less money, but demanded a piece of her soul instead. So she stuck to the old remedy of trying to relieve the pain in her hands with an ice bath rather than selling her soul because of a few blisters.

She'd spent all morning, and most of the afternoon, sewing tiny pieces of glittering white beads onto the bikini top of a Carnival costume. Dianta, the bitchy, blonde girlfriend of Carmella's boss, was the *Rainha da Bateria* of the Ramirez Samba School this year. Dianta's role as the Drum Queen was to march at the front of the samba school drum section during Rio de Janeiro's Carnival parade and showcase herself on behalf of the school. No matter how much Carmella detested the viper-tongued woman, she couldn't bring herself to screw up the costume Dianta would be wearing so that it would have a wardrobe malfunction. She couldn't sabotage Dianta without hurting the school her father had built from the ground up.

Dianta wanted the best costume money could buy, and she wanted Carmella to make it for her because the bitch knew that Carmella couldn't stand her, and she reveled in making Carmella do menial tasks for her amusement.

My father never would have picked her as queen.

She flexed her fingers in the bowl of melting ice and tried to fight back the tears that threatened anytime she thought about her dad. Last year, her father, Gustavo Ramirez, had died in a car accident on his way home after visiting her mother in the hospital. He'd left the samba school to his financial partner, Enrique, who died of food poisoning a few weeks later. The school then passed on to Enrique's son, Miguel, boyfriend to Dianta, minor drug lord, and just all around *desgraçado*.

Fortunately Carmella and her mother kept control of the family estate outside of the city. She was supposed to train under Enrique after she'd graduated college and become part owner of the school someday. Too bad his son had refused to acknowledge this unwritten part of the will. Instead, he acted as if he was doing her a great favor by letting her work at the school as basically his slave. She did all the long, tedious, bullshit jobs and the sewing while he sat on his ass and did coke.

Her father had tried to provide for them after his death, but in a cruel twist of fate, her mother had gotten gravely ill after her father's passing. The life insurance money and inheritance had gone to pay the medical bills from her mother's breast cancer treatments—wiping out pretty much everything they had. Thankfully her mother had been declared cancer free after her double mastectomy, but by then they'd barely had enough money to get by. In an effort to keep her family home, Carmella had to abandon her dreams of an education with only three semesters to go. She'd searched for weeks for a decent job and had been rejected at every turn. When Miguel had offered her a job she'd had no choice and came to work for him as basically an indentured servant.

Sometimes it seemed as though she was cursed with bad luck.

She removed her hands from the ice water and examined the reddened tips of her fingers before drying them on a faded orange towel. Her feet ached too, and she couldn't figure out why. They felt as if she had been dancing for hours in her heels, but she hadn't danced more than two or three times since her father's death. As soon as she started to dance in her father's studio, she'd become overwhelmed with sorrow at the thought that she'd never look up to see him in the floor-to-ceiling mirrors again, so incredibly handsome with her mother in his arms. She'd had the blessing of growing up with parents who truly, deeply loved each other, but it made her own lonely existence hurt all the more.

Rubbing the back of her neck, Carmella walked to the small window over the sink and looked through its bars. The fourth-story apartment peered out over a crowded city block in one of the nicer sections of the ghetto of Rio...if there was such a thing. Clothes hung to dry from lines strewn between the dilapidated apartments, and the sun set over the distant glitter of Rio's skyscrapers.

She lived in an overcrowded section of the city, on the west side of town. It was the only place she could afford and still have enough money to send some home to her mother. Listening to the sounds of the streets coming to life as the sun set, Carmella hummed a tune and twisted her thick, dark hair into a bun. The soft light almost made the view pretty, if one ignored the drug dealers and prostitutes setting up shop across the street. In the far distance, sparkling gold bursts of the nightly fireworks shows put on by alchemists employed by the tourist board began to dot the sky over the coast.

Tiny, but clean, the entire apartment was the size of her bedroom back home. It contained a small kitchen, a bathroom with barely enough room to turn around in, and a living room that doubled as a bedroom. But it was roach-free, and the landlady kept the drug addicts out, so it was good enough for Carmella. Small and safe was better than big and scary, even if she did feel like a scared little rabbit hiding in her apartment at night.

Soon the smell of roasting peppers filled the air as she made dinner. It was lonely eating by herself, but she was embarrassed to invite her old friends to her crappy apartment. The home she'd grown up in was a beautiful ranch house built by her great-great-grandfather. While most of the land had been sold off, they still owned twenty acres that spread out around the dwelling. No matter how much she hated her job, no matter how much she just wanted to quit and run home to her mom, she had no other choice. It was either work for Miguel or lose her house. Her mother still wasn't fully recovered after her long illness and Carmella was pretty sure the shock of losing their ranch would kill her.

Chewing slowly, she tried to make the rice with beans and peppers last. As she ate, her gaze turned to the carved obsidian statue of the Egyptian god, Bes. The image of the squat and bearded dwarf sat on a shelf against the wall, in between pictures of her family and her collection of well-read books. Generations of hands had given the stone a bright, glossy shine. The statue was the last thing her mother had given her before she left home. She thought about the last time she'd seen her mother as she ate her dinner...

"Take it with you. I'm sorry I can't give you more," her mother said with tears in her beautiful dark eyes. Guilt hung in a visible mantle on her frail shoulders, and Carmella ached at the thought of leaving her. "I brought him from Egypt with me when I moved to Brazil as a teenager. He has watched over our family for generations, back to the time of the pharaohs."

Carmella sighed and took the heavy statue of a squat man sticking his tongue out. When she was a little girl she would often amuse herself by sticking her tongue back out at him and making silly faces. That is until the day she swore the statue winked at her when she did it.

"Mama, you know I don't believe in your gods."

Carmella moved the statue to her other arm, the heavy weight pulling at her shoulders. Her attention was caught by a gleam of light off the curve of the statue, drawing her eyes to how much work had gone into making it, and the skill needed to carve such a beautiful piece of art. The stone was smooth like glass beneath her fingers as she traced the curve of a curl in his beard. When she'd glanced up, she could easily read her mother's wish that she take it with her.

"While I'm honored that you're giving me such a valuable piece of my past, I'm not leaving him any tributes. I don't believe in all that nonsense, and I certainly won't be making him honey and milk for breakfast each day. He's not real."

Her mother looked down at the statue and smiled. "Believe what you will, my stubborn daughter. Bes will watch over you and guard you for me. He's the war god of women and children, protecting them from harm and evil." Ignoring Carmella rolling her eyes, she continued in the same patient voice she used for teaching at the samba school. "He loves dancing, drinking, and sensual pleasures. Please, dance for his glory. Leave the other two until you are married."

She took Carmella's hand in her own and gave her a heartbreaking smile. "I fear I can no longer move like I used to. When I was a young girl I celebrated Bes's glory and asked for his blessings by dancing with my mother. Just like we used to dance together when you were a little girl."

Looking down at their joined hands, Carmella marveled at how similar they were. Her skin held more of a golden hue than her mother's dark tan, but the graceful shape of their bone structure was the same. She was a lighter reflection of her mother's dark beauty. The worry in her mother's eyes made her sigh.

"I'll take him with me, Mama, but I won't dance for him. I can't. Not anymore. It hurts too much," Carmella whispered softly as she shifted the heavy weight of the stone to her hip.

"I understand, but remember that the only thing your father loved more than dancing was watching you dance." Her mother sighed and pulled back. "Carmella, I worry about you alone in that big city. Please don't forget we still have friends there. I'm glad Miguel gave you a job as a teacher at the school to earn enough money for college. He's lucky to have you. You're a wonderful dancer, and I just know you'll be the *Rainha da Bateria* this year."

Carmella froze the smile on her face. "Yes, Miguel was very kind. I have to go now, Mama. I love you." It would break her mother's heart if she knew Miguel refused to allow her to teach, only allowing her to do the most menial of tasks.

"I am so proud of you and your father—" She cleared her throat. "Your father would be proud as well. You are my blessing."

****

Carmella sat at the back of the old dance studio, wrapping thin bandages around her fingers. This provided extra protection from the sewing needle, but made the task of holding the tiny glass beads difficult. Her workspace was shoved into the far corner of an old practice room with warped floors that needed replacing, sharing space with props, musical instruments, and cleaning supplies. Racks of bright and sparkly costumes sectioned off the space, giving her enough room to set up a small workbench with her sewing machines and a couple of chairs.

With quick pulls of the needle and thread, she finished the top of Dianta's outfit. Looking over the rim of her clunky black-framed glasses, she admired her work. A sheer tan fabric with hidden cups, it gave the wearer the illusion of having a bare chest while holding the beadwork in place. Intricate snowflakes, more abstract than actual, glittered over the mesh like ice, covering the breasts enough to hide the nipples but little else. Once she was finished, the snowflakes would follow the curve of the waist, flowing in a glittering line down over one hip to meet the bikini bottom.

"Knock knock," said a sensual male voice from the doorway. A moment later Tian poked his head through a rack of costumes, his thick, black hair falling across his forehead. He had the body of a dancer with lean muscles and long legs combined with a killer smile. He was one of the samba school's most popular teachers, and he could bring enough heat to the dance floor to make mothers cover their children's eyes.

"Come on in, handsome." She tied off the bead and bit the string with her teeth. "What brings you to my majestic workspace?"

Tian looked around the tiny section of the room and let out a snort. "I don't know why you put up with this, my *pouco flor*. You know you could move to another city and work at any samba school there. If you won't leave, at least come live with Adam and I. We worry about you living in the ghetto by yourself and wish you would come stay with us."

The apartment Tian shared with his husband was barely bigger than hers and packed with a lot more stuff. She appreciated the gesture, but the idea of sharing one bathroom with two men who took longer to get ready than she did soured the idea. "I'm thankful for the offer—"

"But you don't want to impose, my *pouco flor*," he finished with a small smile.

With a sigh she set down the needle and thread and glared at him. "Stop calling me your little flower. There isn't another city close enough to my mother, and I can't afford a car. She needs me. With my father gone, she has no family left in this country, and she's still recovering from her surgery."

Tossing a stray bead back into the tray so hard it bounced, she vented some of the frustration and despair that was threatening to eat her alive.

"No other samba school in this area will hire me because they don't want to piss off Miguel and without an education I'm nothing." She pushed her glasses back on her nose and tried to control her anger. It shamed her that she'd had to sink so low, and she didn't want to lose his friendship because of her self-disgust. "I'm pretty much stuck."

"I miss watching you dance. You are so beautiful, like a song come to life." His gaze softened as she dashed away a tear, and then he gave her an overly bright smile. "The things you can do with those hips...aye! Your mama's belly dancing skills are in that luscious booty of yours."

Allowing his cheerful banter to wash over her, she snorted and loaded the tip of the needle with beads. With quick pulls of the thread, she resumed her work. "Since you didn't bring me coffee, what reason do you have for interrupting me?" She gave him a wink to take the sting out of her words.

He grabbed an old lawn chair and moved it across from her before taking a seat, turning even that simple move into a dance. "I have some interesting gossip for you. God knows you never leave this depressing little room. Someone has to let you know what's going on in the rest of the world." He ignored her glare and continued, "Miguel has gone off and hired some big name DJ from Europe to ride on our float in the Carnival parade. I heard it cost him buckets of money, and Dianta is sweating off her makeup at the idea of meeting him."

Anger tightened her stomach, along with a burst of envy that Miguel could be so careless with what should be, at least partially, her money while she barely scraped by. "When you deal as many drugs as he does, you can buy whatever you want."

"Lower your voice. The last thing you need is to let Miguel or one of his pets hear you." Tian stood and looked over the racks to make sure no one was around before returning to his seat.

"I've kept my mouth shut, and I know how things work around here," she grumped, resisting the urge to double-check that no one was listening. Her voice dropped to a low whisper. "Miguel has more than enough money to pay off the police. Even if I went to them with all the evidence in the world, I would still end up dead."

"And Miguel would still be free and running around in his cheap imitation designer clothes and terrible taste in cologne," he finished with a sniff.

"Exactly. So I play the good little girl and keep a low profile—and my job." She motioned to her bulky clothes and thick glasses. "I survive by staying under the radar, by not attracting attention to myself."

He was silent for a moment, his usual carefree personality put away. "Is that why you're dressing like a washerwoman? I noticed you're wearing your hair up all the time now with no makeup. And those clothes." He made a disgusted face and plucked at the sleeve of her shirt. "My grandmother wouldn't be caught in them. I can't remember the last time you dressed up like you used to. Where did my Carmella who liked being a beautiful woman go?"

Looking down, Carmella rubbed an old black scuff on the floor with the tip of her shoe. "I got tired of the way Miguel's *business partners* look at me. I'm not one of his samba whores, ready to spread my legs to please his guests." Her stomach clenched and churned at the thought of the sweaty palms of those men pressing against her, leaving a trail of grease on her body.

"Did anyone try to touch you, *pouco flor*?" Tian asked gently.

Carmella shook her head, the ridiculous chunky glasses slipping down her nose. "Not yet, but that tall man with the black cane keeps staring at me. I'll be doing my work and—please don't laugh—I'll feel cold. It's as if the sun has gone behind a cloud and I'm left in the shadows. I know he's in the doorway, watching me, even before I see him." She glanced at Tian to make sure he wasn't laughing at her. "I don't like it. He feels...wrong."

"*Deus nos ajude.*" Tian grimaced as he leaned forward. "Carmella, that's Branco. He's a powerful and very dangerous man. They say he's the priest of a dark god and very big in the black magic world. Stay far away from him. Branco is nothing but trouble."

"I don't mess with the dark gods. Why is he interested in me?" Carmella's hands shook while she tried to continue to sew the costume.

Tian held her trembling hand in his and gave her a smile that didn't reach his worried eyes. "Relax, *flor*. I'm sure he's just being his usual, creepy self. I thank the gods every day Miguel doesn't have any gay business partners." Gesturing to himself in an elegant sweep, he said, "Because this body is not for sale...well, unless Adam and I are role-playing."

Their laughter was interrupted by the sound of heels clicking across the wooden floor. Exchanging a curious glance with Tian, Carmella stood and slid a rack over to the side.

Dianta bounced toward them in all of her silicone and extensions glory. Miguel's girlfriend had come from a rival samba school to the Ramirez School after he'd taken it over. Carmella knew her from the samba dance circuit, and there was no love lost between the two women. Rumor had it Dianta had been caught offering cocaine to some of the samba dancers at her last school to help them stay skinny.

"Here comes the Queen of Fake," Tian whispered in a snarky voice.

Dianta was a plastic surgeon's masterpiece. From her liposuctioned thighs to her fish-pout lips to her bleach-blonde weave, she was a blow-up doll come to life. Carmella could remember when Dianta had been just a mousy little brunette back when they were teenagers. They went to different dance schools at the time and would often compete against each other. *I usually won those competitions without cheating. Dianta was mad enough to chew nails when I won the Samba Queen crown our senior year,* Carmella thought smugly.

That fleeting moment of self-worth quickly vanished under the ever-present cloud of her depression. Not that the crown mattered much now. It sat on a shelf with all her other trophies, collecting dust at her mother's house. She was still a seamstress while Dianta was the pampered and spoiled Drum Queen.

"Carmella, where is my costume? I need it." Dianta walked past Carmella in an overpowering cloud of floral perfume as if she wasn't there and began tossing around pieces of fabric. Her navy blue shorts rode up high enough to be mistaken for panties, and a button-down shirt strained over the amount of silicone in her chest.

"It's not done yet. I—"

Miguel's voice boomed from the hallway. "I think Dianta is in here, working hard on her Carnival costume."

Carmella's jaw dropped as she watched an elegant woman in a stylish purple suit lead a camera crew into the studio. Dianta clenched a random handful of beads and held the top Carmella had just been working on. She even sat in Carmella's chair, poised with the needle in her hand as if she were in mid-stroke.

"Ah, here she is!" Miguel gave the woman next to him a large, false smile. A young man of average height and build, he had an unnatural fondness for multiple gold chains and tight silk pants. His black hair was heavily gelled into spikes, and his teeth were unnaturally white. A pair of gold snakeskin loafers completed the look that Carmella thought of as "early '80s pimp".

"Miguel!" Dianta wiggled out of the chair, an expression of mock surprise stopping at her Botoxed forehead. Her button-down shirt ended below her breasts, and she had somehow made her already giant chest look even bigger. "I didn't know you were here." She batted her long fake lashes and simpered. "Who are these people?"

The woman in the suit smiled at Dianta. "My name is Emma Vinsenz. I'm a reporter with the *Latin Heartbeat,* and we're here from the States doing a story on the *Rainha da Baterias* of this year's Carnival." The woman gave Carmella and Tian a questioning look before turning back to Dianta. "It's very exciting news that DJ Kal is going to be on your float this year. We were wondering if you had some time to talk to us."

"Oh, I don't know if I'm ready enough for the camera. I was just trying to finish some details on my costume. I made it myself." Dianta ducked her head and gave a shy smile that made Carmella want to puke.

Carmella and Tian stood off to the side, staring at Dianta as if she had puppies crawling out of her ears. Miguel noticed them and jerked his head toward the door. The menacing glare he gave them was enough to get Tian moving, even as the rage built inside Carmella almost to the boiling point.

Carmella was about to open her mouth, but Tian hauled her out the door before she could speak. The film crew turned to watch them go, and Miguel distracted them with a joke in his booming voice.

As soon as they were out of sight, Tian clasped his hand over her mouth and continued to drag her toward the back door. She struggled against him and tried to ignore the shocked stares of a group of young students waiting for their class to start. Once outside in the back courtyard, he let go of her and dodged a wild punch she threw at his head.

"That...that...that..." Carmella stuttered out in a series of shouts. She was so angry she was trembling. "How dare she! Who does she think she is!"

Tian leaned against a tree, out of range of her fists. "She knows she's the girlfriend of the owner of the school. She knows she can get away with murder, and she knows you won't speak up for fear of losing your job."

"I should go back in there and tell them I made that costume! I designed it, I picked out the theme, I sewed all ten fucking thousand beads on it by hand, and I have the sore fingers to prove it!" Carmella finished, thrusting her bandaged hand into the warm and muggy afternoon air.

"That may be, *pouco flor*, but do you really want to lose your job here because of one bitch? Miguel will tire of her soon and move onto some new coke whore." Tian pulled her in close for a hug, resting his head on top of her dark hair. "There are many people here who worked for your father and helped him build this samba school that still love you. We're just hoping you will outlive Miguel and take over when he gets shot by some drug lord."

"Don't hold your breath. That man is a cockroach." Carmella sniffed against his shirt.

"A cockroach he may be, but we can always hope he annoys someone with a big enough shoe to stomp him."

"You say the sweetest things, Tian." Anger still burned through her, but the darkness of her depression smothered it beneath a wave of doubt. Tian was right; there was nothing she could do to change her situation. She was a nobody, and the camera crew would just laugh at her if she spoke up.

"I know, *flor*. Now let's go wash your face and grab a bite to eat. Then you'll finish that bitch's costume. Try to sew the crotch so it will pinch her down below." He put a finger to his lips. "Wait, that area has probably seen so much use it's numb. Try making it pinch her hips instead."

****

Carmella woke in the middle of the night with a racing heart and aching limbs. The horrible nightmare had left a foul taste in her mouth that seemed to curdle against her lips. It was the same dream that had been repeating itself for the last two weeks and leaving her fearful and covered in oily sweat when she awoke.

In it, she wandered down an alley at night, holding a man's hand. The face and clothes of the man changed with each dream, but the destination was always the same. She took them to the front door of a bar. The sign above it was white neon in the shape of two giant dice. The man would usually stand behind her, docile as a lamb. With no control of her body, she would watch her hand rap a strange rhythm on the door. Bracelets glittered on her wrists, and an unfamiliar tight and silky red dress clung to her curves.

The door would open, and there would be only darkness beyond. She would find herself frozen, unable to look away from the blackness that seemed to throb out into the alley.

Sometimes the man behind her would scream; other times he would shout and try to pull her away.

Just before the darkness revealed... something terrible... she would wake up.

It didn't make any sense. She didn't own a pair of high heels like ones she wore in the dream. Heck, she wasn't even sure she could walk in six-inch heels, let alone saunter down an alley. In these nightmares she always wore the same slutty red dress, an outfit she was sure she'd never owned let alone wore. Usually she stuck to flowing sundresses on the rare occasion that she went out, not skintight crimson silk. There was no rhyme or reason why her subconscious was stuck on this dream, but she was really getting tired of constantly reliving the nightmare.

With a sigh, she rolled over and tried to go back to sleep. Whenever she had this dream, she was always exhausted the next day, no matter how many hours she slept. As her eyes closed, she curled into a tight ball beneath her quilt, afraid of what was hiding in the dark.

CHAPTER THREE

With a small growl, Carmella jerked the edges of the plastic bag open and white feathers of every shape and size flew into the air. For a moment, she sat in the patch of late morning sun, watching the soft cloud of white float to the ground. It was so tempting to just give up, to return to her apartment and never leave again. A memory of her mother's love brushed against her, and she found the strength to push back the despair. Muttering a colorful blend of curse words in two languages, Carmella knelt and began to gather the feathers into a pile on the floor of her small workspace.

Tian chose that moment to poke his head over the racks. "What in the world! Carmella, are you slaughtering chickens back here? I admire your wish to do harm to Dianta, but really, voodoo is not the way to go."

Carmella gave Tian a nasty look from over the top of her glasses. "Instead of standing there watching me, why don't you come help? Or maybe I will start doing voodoo, and you'll be the first doll I make."

Clucking his tongue, Tian removed a feather from her shoulder. "Your glare would be much more effective if you didn't look like a molting goose."

Blowing stray pieces of hair off her forehead, Carmella slumped on the floor. "I'm sorry, Tian. I saw Dianta on TV this morning, and it put me in a bad mood for the rest of the day."

What she didn't tell Tian was that when she'd awoken this morning, there was this feeling in her heart—in her soul—that today was going to be a wonderful day. The sun seemed brighter as it filtered through her thrift store curtains. Even the motes of dust floating in the beams of light seemed magical. Her oatmeal and raisins tasted better than she ever remembered, and the sounds coming from the street seemed more like music than noise. That feeling of blissful expectation ended quickly when she saw Dianta simpering and strutting her way through the morning news on Carmella's old television.

Tian sighed. "I understand. Adam and I watched her during breakfast. Could you believe the lies coming out of that woman's mouth? Saying she found time to sew her costume between doing charity work at a local soup kitchen and rescuing stray cats."

"I know. I kept waiting for her to add something about saving orphans from a burning building."

"Or giving CPR to dying grandmothers. Please, can you imagine her trying to do anything with those three-inch fake nails of hers?"

Carmella hugged the bag of feathers to her chest, little puffs of down flying out from the open top. "It just makes me so mad. Why can't there be more people in this world with integrity? Why am I surrounded by such low-class filth?" Catching Tian's snarky look, she amended, "Present company excluded, of course."

"Thank you." Tian helped her gather the feathers as she plucked them off her shirt. "The DJ that's coming, DJ Kal I think his name is, Adam said he does all kinds of charity work. Mainly with free hospitals and clinics."

"I wish we had something like that down here. Our hospital system is strained to the limit. That's why we had to pay so much to take my mother to a private clinic."

Tian kissed the top of her head. "You're a good daughter. You have to believe there are other people with integrity and honor like yours out there."

"Yeah, well, it would be nice if the gods would help them find me. I need...something to believe in again, and to believe in me. Why can't I find one decent guy in this city?" Carmella sighed.

"Because they are all either gay or married," Tian said with a sunny smile.

Carmella stuck her tongue out at him. "I'm sorry to get so melodramatic with you. I didn't sleep well last night, and that makes me cranky." She bit her lip and tried to forget the nightmares that dominated her dreams.

"Well, you don't have time to be cranky right now. We have to get to the main practice hall too. Miguel and Dianta are meeting with DJ Kal this morning, and they want to parade us around in front of him." Tian stood, checking his dark blue pants for feathers.

"Crap, I forgot about that. Do you think they'll notice if I'm not there?"

"Yep, if it'll give them an excuse to yell at you. Just come with me, and we'll make nice to the DJ. If you can keep yourself from punching Dianta, I'll buy you lunch." Tian stretched and grinned at her.

She set the bag down and brushed the feathers from her cargo pants. Despite the heat, she wore clothing that covered her from head to toe. Baggy black shirt, baggy brown pants, big fake glasses and her hair back in a bun all worked to disguise her femininity.

A brief brush of the happiness from the morning touched her soul, and she wished she had worn something nicer. Maybe one of the brightly colored tank tops that she used to wear to school. Men had always complimented her in them. That thought was squashed by the need to remain invisible to Miguel and his business associates. Especially Branco, with his silent feet and dark stare.

Tian gave her a precise bow that snapped her out of her morose thoughts. "Are you ready, my *flor*?"

Lowering her lashes, she bent into a graceful curtsey, her movements flowing and liquid. "Of course, my handsome escort. Shall we?"

He spun her in a whip-quick circle, her feet easily moving in a tight loop as she twirled in his arms. "I miss dancing with you, and I miss your laughter even more." He placed a kiss on her forehead. "When you feel like being alive again, promise me we will go dancing."

She sighed and strolled down the hallway with Tian. "I don't know what can resurrect me, Tian. My soul feels like it's locked in ice."

"The sun will find you. Have faith." Tian threw an arm over her shoulder and tugged her close.

Nodding, she didn't bother to reply. Instead, she sent another silent prayer. *Please, anyone, if you're listening...please help me be warm again.*

The large domed auditorium, with its white walls and pale wood floor, echoed with hundreds of excited voices. The entire staff, and most of the students of the samba school, stood around and chatted. Anticipation filled the air as they waited for Miguel and the DJ to arrive.

Carmella stayed at the back of the room and tugged at her too-long shirt. She tried to avoid the people who had worked at the school when her father was alive. They made her remember how wonderful things used to be here, and she felt guilty for avoiding them now that Miguel owned the school. In her heart, she knew they were good people who cared about her, but they were just as helpless in this situation as she was. Everyone needed their job. With unemployment as high as it was in Rio, any honest work was sought after and fought over.

Fatima, a dance instructor and old friend, moved through the group to speak to her. "Aren't you excited, Carmella?"

Fatima wore a bright pink top embroidered with glittering blue sequins that practically glowed. Blinking against the intense color, Carmella pushed her glasses on top of her head. "Not really. I won't be in the parade this year. As long as Dianta looks fabulous, I've done my job." She concentrated on rolling her sleeves up to try to control her emotions. They were so close to the surface today, and after months of feeling nothing, she found the sensation disconcerting. Life was bearable because she didn't feel, didn't hope for anything more than what she had.

Looking crestfallen, Fatima bit her lip. "I'm so sorry. Me and my big mouth." Giving the crowd a furtive glance, Fatima lowered her voice and stepped closer. "It's a crime that you're not dancing with us. All the instructors agree that you should be the Drum Queen. I think Dianta is just jealous of you. That's why she forbade Miguel from hiring you as a samba instructor and made you her seamstress instead."

Carmella felt her jaw drop as her breath came out in a harsh gasp. Anger grew to fury, and her head throbbed with a sudden sharp ache. She grabbed Fatima's hand and dragged her back against the wall. "Dianta forbade it? I thought Miguel made that decision!"

Fatima tugged her hand away and glanced around the room. "I thought you knew. Dianta considers you her main competition here and would never stand for you outshining her. Don't think for a moment she forgot you won most of the dance crowns when you were teenagers." The sparkles on Fatima's shirt glittered as she leaned in even closer. "She would be happy if you never came back, but Miguel wants you around so he can still use the Ramirez name." She lowered her voice further until it was barely more than a movement of her lips, "Her little lapdogs are watching us. I'm so sorry, but I must go."

Pretending to rub her chin on her shoulder, Carmella noted two of Dianta's favorite students, and fellow cokeheads, watching them. "Thank you so much for letting me borrow that DJ Kal CD, Fatima. I don't have any of his music. I would feel so silly if anyone asked me about him and I didn't know a single song."

Fatima gave her a grateful look. "No problem, Carmella. It's in the CD player in my studio. Feel free to grab it anytime you want."

Carmella nodded and stared at the far wall of the room while clenching her fists. The nerve of Dianta. How dare she forbid her from teaching out of petty jealousy? This wasn't high school. She needed the extra money teaching would provide to survive. The throbbing in her head increased, and she placed her hands over her eyes in an effort to stave off a full-blown migraine.

Trying to calm herself, she didn't even notice the double doors of the room opening. It wasn't until Miguel's loud voice rang through the rafters that she looked up.

Miguel led a husky man with a shaggy mop of brown hair into the room and gestured to the crowd with a proud smile. Dianta snuggled next to him and whispered something in his ear. It took all of Carmella's willpower not to go over there and tug Dianta's weave right off her head.

She made her way through the crowd to stand next to Tian. The anger had cleared her mind, giving her a sense of clarity and focus that she hadn't even realized was missing. "That's the world-famous DJ?"

"No, that's his crew manager. There he is, Sean Kalmus, a.k.a. DJ Kal."

She caught sight of him, and her breath stuck in her throat. He was magnificent. Tall, he wore an off-white shirt that clung to his broad shoulders and powerful chest. Long legs, thick with muscle, filled out his jeans, and he had the graceful fingers of an artist. She couldn't see his face from this angle, only the blaze of his red-brown hair and the line of his strong jaw.

"He doesn't walk like a musician," Tian murmured in her ear. "He walks like a fighter."

All Carmella could do was nod. Time seemed to slow down, and the crowd around her faded to insignificance. She could see every nuance of his movements, and the timbre of his distant voice made her want to sigh. Her body went from hot to cold and back to hot again as she waited for Sean to turn around. She had to see his eyes. Once she saw his eyes she would know him and would be able to taste his spirit.

Dianta pranced around them, her teased blonde hair blocking his face from view. Impatiently, Carmella pushed her way to the front of the crowd. There were grumbles and complaints as she elbowed through, but none of that mattered. She had to see him.

Miguel's speech about the glory of the school washed over her like meaningless babble. She considered breaking rank and walking to him herself just before he finally turned. At the first sight of his amazing blue eyes, her world shifted on its axis.

The pounding of her heart drowned out the voices around her. Gods, he was handsome. His face was all masculine angles, wonderful blends of shadows and light. And his eyes, his eyes were overwhelming, a dark gray-blue that reminded her of the sea during a storm. Hard eyes, dominating eyes, but filled with kindness and compassion behind all his strength.

Energy filled her, reawakening the blissful feeling from this morning of impending joy. She scarcely dared to breathe, her gaze locked on his face. As Miguel talked, Sean scanned the large crowd of dancers and musicians, lowering his head to speak to the shaggy-haired man every now and then.

Sean seemed to be avoiding Dianta. She would bounce in his direction, and he would subtly turn his body away from her. It was funny watching him give her the cold shoulder. At one point, he even avoided a clutching manicured claw in a move a ninja would envy. Carmella couldn't help but a smirk of satisfaction over Dianta's increasingly desperate attempts to attract his attention.

Impatiently, she waited for his attention to reach her part of the crowd. A small part of her mind told her to hide, that she was worthless and would embarrass herself if he did notice her. Her soul told it to shut up.

Sean caught her eye, and she swore his jaw dropped. A small smile began to bloom on her lips but quickly wilted as he turned to speak with the shaggy man. Sean's mouth lifted in a curl of disgust when Miguel laid a hand on his shoulder. Miguel didn't seem to notice, but Carmella could see Sean's body stiffen as he moved away from Miguel.

Feeling like a fool, she moved quickly to the back of the crowd and hid behind Tian. What was she thinking? Why would he be interested in a mouse of a woman dressed in clothes three times her size? He was beyond anything she had ever seen. He must have women throwing themselves at him. Dianta had certainly tried every trick in her slutty book to gain his attention. Miguel kept attempting to casually move her away from Sean, to the point of securing an arm around her waist and pinning her to his side.

Carmella wallowed in her misery. If only things were different. If only her father was still alive and she stood next to Sean, welcoming him. She wanted to go crawl in a hole and hide. In front of the entire school she had stared at him like some love struck teenager. Tian gave her a curious look, but left her alone as the squad divisions and song choices were explained.

Wrapped in her depression, she stared out the window at the busy street. She wished with all her heart that her father had never died, that her mother had never gotten sick, and she was still the girl who believed in fairy tales.

"You have something in your hair," a voice cloaked in a wonderful accent said.

Carmella turned so quickly she nearly gave herself whiplash. Sean stood not three feet from her, an amused smile curving his lips. The sunlight burned through his red hair like fire, and it caught the fine light red stubble on his face. This close, he stunned her with his presence, and all she could do was stare. She found herself turning toward him, like a flower following the sun.

"I'm sorry." Sean raised a fair eyebrow. "Do you speak English?"

"Oh, yes, I do. I'm sorry, what did you say?" Carmella breathed out, feeling like a fool, but unable to focus her thoughts when he was this close.

Sean walked toward her and reached up, plucking a few bits of white down feathers from her bun. She wanted a hole in the floor to open so she could jump into it. She also wanted to grab his large hand and place gentle kisses on his palm before sliding it down her willing body. Realizing everyone was staring at her, Carmella blushed all the harder. "I was sewing some feathers on to the Winter Queen costume. I....uh...had a mishap with the bag."

Tian held a hand over his mouth behind Sean's back, laughing at her.

Sean gently pulled a few more feathers from her dark bun. That simple act felt like a gentle caress, and her body responded with a flush of heat. The soft flesh between her legs began to flood with warmth, and she had a distracted thought that it had been forever since she felt any desire.

He seemed to linger as he pulled the feathers out, gently pulling and smoothing her hair. Those long fingers moved with such grace he could probably play her body like an instrument. Desire flowed through her blood, making her skin sensitive to the slightest breeze. Looking into his storm-blue eyes, she wondered what color they turned when he was in the grip of passion.

"What is your name, little bird?" he asked as he brushed his hands together. His voice was kind, and he was careful not to invade her space.

"I'm little flower." He looked sharply as if she'd said something obscene. That made her blush even harder. "I mean, my name is Carmella Ramirez. Please ignore the nickname. I didn't get much sleep last night." She mentally scolded herself for acting like a flake as Tian turned an alarming shade of red while holding back his laughter behind Sean.

Sean raised his hand toward her face, and Dianta appeared out of nowhere. She snatched his hand out of the air with a brittle smile. "Sean, there you are, you handsome man." She tugged him toward Miguel, waiting for them at the entrance. "I see you've met one of our seamstresses. I do hope she hasn't bored you too much."

Turning to Carmella, Dianta gave her a frozen smile and waved her manicured fingers at her in a shooing gesture. "Run along now, Carmella. Stop bothering Mr. Kalmus. I don't know why you're here anyway. It's not like you're going to dance in the Carnival." She let out a mean little titter and snuggled against Sean's side.

Carmella's lower lip trembled at the angry look on Sean's face. He must have thought she was a dancer. His disappointment cut her like a knife, and she turned quickly and left, not wanting Sean to see the tears filling her eyes.

Damn that woman, he was *hers*.

The thought stopped her cold. What in the world was wrong with her? He was a stranger, an extremely gorgeous stranger, but a stranger nonetheless. She had no claim on him. All he did was come over and pull feathers out of her hair. Ignoring the curious looks from the people she passed in the hall, she went into Fatima's dance studio and shut the door with a slam.

Her emotions were out of control, and she wanted to scream at the top of her lungs. Not a violent person by nature, the rapidly escalating rage filled her with terror and she took a shaky breath, striving to regain control of her emotions. This wasn't like her. Maybe she was losing her mind. Eyes closing, she slumped into the corner and let the tears finally fall.

Chapter Four

Sean kept his voice low as he and Kell lounged on a rough picnic bench in the small courtyard behind the samba school. A banana tree arched overhead, providing a small patch of shade. The fierce Brazilian sun beat down on the courtyard and turned it into an oven, and Sean wiped the sweat off his forehead. Kell smoked a fragrant hand-rolled cigarette, their excuse for getting away from Dianta's endless chatter and Miguel's glowering looks.

"This place stinks of evil," Kell muttered in a low voice. "What have you been able to figure out?"

They could have used an auditory shield spell, but Sean didn't want Miguel to know he knew magic. Something was going on here. He'd first sensed it when Miguel and Dianta met him at the hotel. Both of their auras were tainted with darkness that left a smear of psychic filth. They had been doing some heavy black magic to get that much evil on their souls.

Sean kept his shields tight. Even if Miguel could see auras, a rare ability, all he would see of Sean's was the outer edges. Hidden inside his aura were the streaks of slow gold lightning that marked him as Chosen. Anyone with a trained eye who saw that would know he had a personal relationship with his patron god, and that made him dangerous.

Switching to Gaelic, Sean said, "Most of the students here are normal humans and nothing special. The staff is another matter. A few are still free of the taint of darkness, but most have at least been brushed with it. The women especially."

"What about that walking blow-up doll, Dianta?" Kell spat a loose piece of tobacco on the ground.

"Bad. Her psychic smell is like garbage rotting in the sun. Miguel isn't much better, but he seems weak somehow. I think Dianta is the real power of this place...or at least a portion of it. I can't imagine her being smart enough to learn high magic."

Kell tapped the ash from his cigarette on the ground. "What's up with that homely little thing you were talking with? I don't think anyone, well, other than Dianta, noticed you couldn't keep your eyes off her. Did I miss something?"

Sean stared at Kell. How could he call Carmella homely? Didn't he notice her lovely skin, its soft tone more gold than tan. And her movements...even running out the door she reminded him of a graceful cat. Though she tried to hide it, the lush body beneath her clothing had made his cock hard the moment he saw her.

But it was more than just looks. Her aura was a stunning violet with a soft sparkling gold mist rising from it. He didn't know who her god was, but that mist on her aura was a clear sign she was considered a favorite.

"I think she's my first flower of spring." Sean grinned at Kell's incredulous look. "She had 'snow' in her hair in the form of feathers, and her nickname is little flower. And her aura, it's a beautiful purple, like the first violets of spring. She has such a gentle soul."

Staring at him, Kell began to laugh. "Oh man. Sean, you're twitterpated over this girl."

Sean narrowed his eyes at Kell. "I am not twitterpated. I..." He paused for a second and felt an unfamiliar grin lift his lips. It almost felt silly. "I think she's my *Comhcheol*."

Letting out a low whistle, Kell looked at him closely as he ran a hand over his dark brown hair. "Shit, that complicates things." Kell also turned to look at the building as if he could see the girl inside. "So, she's your harmony. That special soul that resonates with your own. Hell of a time to find her."

Sean nodded, all thoughts of evil and Carnivals gone from his mind as he embraced the possibility. It was a rare thing to find one's *Comhcheol* and considered a great blessing from the gods when it happened. He sent a silent prayer of thanks to his god, Maponus, for bringing him here.

Snapping his fingers in Sean's face, Kell said, "Well, your little flower is in a samba school that is being used for some kind of demonic magic. You need to worry about what is going on and how it might be affecting your lady before you two start picking out curtains."

Sean clenched his fists at the thought of Carmella coming to any harm. "You're right. Let's get back inside and see what Dianta and Miguel want us to do for the Carnival. We still need to coordinate our theater troupe with their musicians and dancers. No reason to let them know we're suspicious."

Standing and pulling his damp shirt from his back, Sean said, "Tomorrow I'm going to have Monica and Whitney come in and work with their choreographers. We need to keep everything as normal as possible, and I still have that charity DJ gig tomorrow night. Warn everyone to wear protection charms before they come to this school and to always stay with at least one other member of our troupe."

Kell ground out the cigarette butt into the dust with his boot. "No rest for the weary, my friend."

****

Carmella didn't want to leave the peaceful solitude of the dance studio. She hadn't been inside this room since her father passed away.

It used to be one of her favorite practice spaces with its polished wood floors and soft butterscotch-painted walls. As a child, she'd spent endless hours watching her father teach the samba, the carimbó and the lundu. Some of her favorite memories were of watching her father and mother twirling together in these mirrors.

If she was really good and promised to stay quiet, they would let her watch the carimbó practice. It was a sensual dance with a woman and a man seeking to seduce each other on the floor. Dressed in white shirts and pants with bright red strips of cloth as belts, the men looked so dashing to her young eyes.

The women wore long flowing skirts with brightly colored designs. They would flip the skirts at their male partners, twirling and using the cloth as an extension of their bodies. She loved the costumes. It was part of the reason she'd begged the school's old seamstress to teach her to sew.

Watching herself in the mirror, she began to dance, really dance, for the first time since her father died. She started slow, a few turns, an arc of the arms. With a frown, she took off her bulky shirt and tossed it in the corner. Standing at the barre at the back of the wall, she began to go through her stretching routine. Her body remembered the moves. They were so ingrained she could do them in her sleep. Muscles woke and protested as her tendons warmed up and her heart beat faster to rush oxygen through her blood.

Clad in a white tank top and her sports bra, she smiled at her reflection and did a couple of lightning-fast turns. Her baggy pants rode low, leaving an inch of her lower stomach and the top curves of her hips sticking out. The sight of her protruding hipbones brought a momentary flash of dismay. When had she gotten so skinny? She didn't remember looking into the mirror and seeing so much bone. In fact, she couldn't think of the last time she had looked at her body.

Taking in a deep lungful of air, she could almost smell the sharp spice of her father's cologne in the air, as if it had become a part of the room. How he had loved to dance. Snapping her fingers, she wished she had musicians here to give her a beat. The need to move filled her until she practically vibrated with energy. The pain in her soul could be cleansed with the fire of dance. Flexing her feet and rotating her ankles, she looked through the collection of CDs Fatima kept on top of the sound system.

Carmella smiled and pulled out one of Sean's CDs. On the cover, a large tree beneath a night sky gave shelter to a sleeping child. The title was *Dreams of Innocence*. Flipping over to the back, she sucked in her breath as a picture of Sean held her gaze. He was looking through the fringe of his fair lashes with a devilish smile quirking his lips. His hands were placed on a complicated turntable, and the background was a misty forest. The more she stared at his picture, the more it seemed as though he was looking right back at her.

A whisper of desire moved through her as she examined his lips. Not as full as hers, they were firm and well shaped. Her nipples hardened into aching tips as she imagined what it would be like to kiss him, to lick the top curve of his mouth. Would he taste cold and fresh like the ocean where he was from?

Too distracted by his image to read the titles of the songs, she slipped the CD in and played one at random. Her heart swelled as the music drifted from the speakers. It was a belly dancing song, similar to the ones her mother used to play when she danced. At first, it was just an introduction of drums, clean and simple, powerful. Then a woman's voice flowed in, blending with the drums. Finally, Sean began to spin, mixing synthetic melodies and bass beats into an intoxicating rhythm.

Carmella watched herself in the mirror. Light filled her eyes, and her chest rose and fell as her breathing accelerated. The hard tips of her nipples stuck out through the thin cotton of her shirt, and her pulse visibly throbbed in her throat. Her imagination took over, and she could see Sean spinning this music, could feel him in the echo of the base through her bones.

The raw emotion and need she saw in her face was too much for her. Closing her eyes, she let the music take her. It filled her limbs, made them light as air and full of energy. A deep throb settled itself into her hips, grounding her feet with its strength.

Lifting her arms in front of her, she began to dance with a careful flexing of the fingers, flowing in a wave down her arms. Isolating her chest, she gave a pop of movement, rolling it down her stomach in a controlled undulation of muscle to her hips. Briefly, she wished she was wearing a belled scarf to chime around her hips, but the music took hold of her again.

Eyes closed, one with the beat, she let it lead her in the dance. Faster bass now, a fixed shimmy with her hips, shifting her weight to her back as she rolled her lower body in a tight figure eight. Cleansing, purifying, the music moved her across the room, her arms arching and a sweat breaking out over her skin.

In her mind, she danced for Sean. Enticing him with the flash of her hair, seducing him with the arch of her back. Each move and breath done to show him what she had to offer, what could be his if he had the courage to approach her.

The song began to wind down, the bass backing off, the woman's voice left on its own. She followed the simple melody, isolating her stomach muscles as she shimmied her chest. For a moment, she enjoyed the breath panting out of her body, the buzz of her muscles, and the endorphin rush.

Clapping broke the silence, and her eyes flew open in shock. Reflected in the mirror was Sean and his crew manager, both smiling and clapping. She stared at them with an embarrassed blush blending in with the flush of her cheeks. Her mortification once again turned her into an insecure mess. Emotions fought within her, the darkness of depression struggling to reassert itself against the newfound heat of her desire.

"I'm so sorry. I didn't mean to play the music so loud. Please forgive me, I didn't mean to disturb you," she babbled out and twisted her hands behind her back.

The shaggy man looked puzzled, but Sean gave her a smile that made her heart pause a beat then thump all the harder. Sweat trickled down the side of her face, and she dashed it away.

"Carmella, you're an amazing dancer. I am honored that one of my songs inspired you to move like that," Sean said in his lovely accent. The way his eyes went soft when he said her name made her smile back at him with real warmth.

He remembered my name! The silly teenage girl inside her giggled. Carmella tried to scold herself for getting so worked up over such a simple thing, but the giggly teenager wouldn't stop. *He thinks I'm an amazing dancer too!* Happiness filled her heart as she locked her gaze with Sean's. He was smiling at her as if she was the most wonderful thing he had ever seen. It had been a long, long time since anyone had looked at her like this, and she bathed in the heat of his gaze.

The other man looked at Sean and muttered, "Twitterpated," and seemed to smirk. *Must be an Irish word,* Carmella thought absently as Sean continued to smile at her with that heart-stopping look in his eyes. They stared at each other, their breaths unconsciously slowing and matching each other until the rise and fall of their chests became one.

The shaggy man poked Sean in the ribs. "You're a lovely dancer. Monica, our choreographer, should talk to you when she comes to visit tomorrow. I know we're here for the samba, but you've got some belly dancing moves that she would kill to learn."

The darkness inside of her flexed, and images of Sean's choreographers laughing at her filled her mind. She felt the smile wilt off her face, and her gaze fell from Sean to the floor. She couldn't teach a professional choreographer. She was just a seamstress, not even good enough to teach the beginners class at the school. Monica would laugh in her face when she saw her pitiful attempts at dancing and tell Sean how horrible she was.

Sean's blue eyes darkened, and he took a step toward her. Before he could touch her, she ducked from beneath his hand and backed away from him. "I'm sorry, I can't. If you'll please excuse me, I have to finish Dianta's costume." For the second time today, she found herself running away from Sean.

****

The breeze generated by her ancient rotating fan did little to cool Carmella. Back in her cramped studio, the afternoon sun blazed through the windows and turned the room into an oven. While the rest of the individual practice rooms were air-conditioned, her room was in an older part of the building that had never been upgraded. Usually she took her work to one of the unoccupied practice rooms, but with Carnival coming up the samba school was buzzing with activity and she'd been stuck in her cramped and hot workspace.

Sean and his people were everywhere. Unfamiliar faces and accents filled the hallway outside of her studio with laughter and energy. The darkness that seemed to hang over her had lifted, and everyone seemed happier. Everyone except her.

Tian had let her know that Sean was looking for her, but she had begged him to cover for her, claiming that she wasn't feeling well. He had given her an odd look, but promised not to tell Sean where she was. And now she sat, sweating and hiding from the man who hadn't left her thoughts since meeting him.

She wanted so badly to find Sean, to apologize for running away from him. Every time she almost got up the nerve to go find him, she'd look down at hands with her nails bitten off to the quick and chickened out. He'd probably just been being nice to her, feeling sorry for her obvious lack of grace and sophistication. There was no way a man, who had his pick of gorgeous and fascinating women, would ever want anything to do with her.

She had spied on him this morning, watched him enter the school flanked by amazingly confident and beautiful women. Her heart had ached when she saw the easy way they all talked together, how he had laughed at something they said and given one of the women a quick hug. If the devil had claimed her soul in exchange for taking the place of the woman in Sean's arms, she would have happily given it. That was about the only way she would ever feel his embrace.

She was so absorbed in feeling sorry for herself that she didn't respond to the knock on the door. It was only after the person on the other side gave a good pound that she surfaced from the darkness inside of her and set aside the costume she worked on. After wiping the sweat off her face with the edge of her shirt, she yelled, "Come in!"

Time stopped as the door swung open, and Sean strode into the room holding a white paper bag. The sunlight hit his hair, bringing out the red and gold highlights in a blaze of color. His storm-gray eyes found hers, and a smile lit his face. Happy, he was actually happy to see her. So handsome, he was even more amazing than she remembered.

"Hello, Carmella. I hope you don't mind that I stopped by. Tian said you weren't feeling well." She stared at him in silence, and his smile turned uncertain. "I, uh, thought you might like a drink."

Her mind refused to process his words. "Drink?"

"Yeah. Tian said your stomach was upset, and I thought maybe a cold drink would help.

This heat is brutal. I was afraid you might be getting dehydrated." He scooted around a rack of costumes and took a quick glance around. A hard look of anger and disgust crossed his face, and she immediately felt ashamed. "How can you work in here? It's so hot I can barely breathe."

Looking only at her hands, she shrugged. "You get used to it." She was not going to tell him that usually she worked in here at night, spending the heat of the day in one of the empty practice rooms. Then he would ask her why she'd stayed in here today, and she would have to lie to him. For some reason, the thought of lying to Sean made her feel ill.

The silence between them deepened, and she could feel his tension and anger. It must have been her imagination, but she swore she would have been able to find him in the middle of the night at the bottom of a mineshaft. It was as if her body responded to his like a flower turning to find the sun.

The paper sack rustled, and something cold pressed up against her neck. She shrieked and grabbed at the icy can of soda. Her body broke out in goose bumps as Sean laughed. She wasn't sure if it was from the shocking cold or the sound of his laughter. It had an almost musical quality that radiated joy.

Daring to glance up at him, she saw that he watched her with an amused smile. Before she could look away, his gaze captured hers, and she lost herself in his eyes. Different shades of gray and blue moved through them like a stormy sea, and she became entranced. The deeper she looked, the more she saw until his gaze became her world.

His voice, deep and mellow, moved through her blood and sent sparks of pleasure flickering through her nervous system. "Carmella, you're going to teach me how to dance today."

The instant panic his request, no his demand, triggered was washed away as he held her gaze and she found herself cocooned by the power of his will. "Okay." Anything he asked of her would be okay. Warmth and desire swam through the depths of his stare, and her body heated in response. The feeling of desire was almost shocking after having been without it for so long. The last time she'd been on a date was before her father had passed and her body was starved for affection. Her nipples hardened to aching points, and she licked her suddenly sensitive lips. His gaze followed her tongue, and a wave of lust washed over her.

Clearing his throat, he turned his back and fumbled with the bag, breaking his hold on her. She almost dropped the soda she was holding as reality came rushing back in. What was she doing? She couldn't teach him how to dance. The very idea was ludicrous.

With his back still to her, he said in a rough and husky voice, "Let's go."

He turned and held his hand out to her. Despite her mind's protests, her body knew what it wanted. Setting the can on the floor, she slipped her hand into his and almost gasped. Energy flowed between them, and a hint of deep green streaked with gold appeared around Sean for a moment. It took her a moment to realize she was seeing Sean's aura and she couldn't stop the small gasp of wonder that escaped her.

Normally she didn't have the talent or magical ability needed to see the energy that surrounded every living creature, but with Sean she could see it as clearly as if she gazed through a pair of outrageously expensive second sight glasses. The deep, vibrant green wrapped around her and caressed against her body in a way that set her blood on fire. Her hips arched forward as a low ache settled deep into her pussy. The energy condensed until it felt as if phantom lips were trailing over her neck. Sean let out a barely audible groan, and abruptly the sensation was gone, and she was alone in her body again.

Blinking rapidly, she would have pulled away if his hand hadn't held hers so tight. He gave her a small, bemused smile. "Sorry about that. My aura likes you. Let's get out of here before it decides to misbehave again."

Not trusting herself to speak, she just nodded as if she understood and let him lead her out of the room. She had no idea what had just happened between them, but she did know that it had been one of the most exciting moments of her life. She felt so alive, so aware, and relished the sensation of his large hand holding hers. An echo of—*what did he call it?*—his aura moved over her, and he glanced over his shoulder to give her a wicked grin.

As soon as they stepped into the hall, whispers erupted at the sight of them holding hands. Students gathered around one of the water coolers stared at them with disbelief. At the other end of the hall, a small cluster of teachers openly gaped. Sean ignored them all and led her to one of the practice rooms.

A hot flush burned her cheeks as the door closed behind them. The cool air felt wonderful on her overheated skin. Still pulling her after him, Sean went to the sound system against the wall and hit play.

Deep drums pulsed out their bass rhythm as he finally spoke. "I was hoping you could teach me some of Brazil's traditional dances. While I won't be dancing in the parade, I do need to know how you move in order to set my music to the right beat."

Clearing her throat, she tried to tug her hand out of his, but he held on. "Why are you asking me? You should speak to one of our instructors. I'm just the seamstress." She looked beyond his shoulder to the wall, not wanting to look at him and see his disappointment.

"Carmella," goodness, she loved how he said her name. "You will never be just a seamstress."

"What?"

He tugged her over to the floor-to-ceiling mirrors and placed her in front of him. She looked away, unable to deal with the sight of them standing together. It did no good; she could still see the image in her mind of a frumpy woman next to a gloriously handsome man. She'd taken off her sweatshirt earlier due to the heat of her workspace and her erect nipples were clearly visible through her faded and worn t-shirt. The top of her head came up to just below his jaw, and she looked so delicate and tiny next to his muscled frame. Dark and light, they complemented each other. She couldn't describe it, but he seemed to somehow shelter her with his body, to curve around and embrace her, even when she was just standing in front of him.

With a gentle touch, he smoothed a stray strand of her hair off her ear and whispered, "You might try to hide yourself beneath those clothes, but you will never be anything other than what you already are. Beautiful."

The feeling of his breath tickling against her ear had her heart slamming into her ribs. He pulled her closer until her back pressed into his chest. The smell of his cologne washed over her, clean and crisp with a faint musk. Her nostrils flared to take his scent deep into her body even as she stiffened against him. This couldn't be happening, couldn't really be true. She must have passed out in her studio from the heat and was having some kind of delusion right now.

He began to rock behind her, pulling her body into the music. Keeping her gaze on the floor, she relaxed enough to let him lead her movements. The way he became one with the drumbeats was amazing. He led her in perfect rhythm, as if his body was an extension of the music. Her heart pounded as his hips brushed against her bottom, and she felt his erection. Hard and impossible to ignore, she bit back a moan as his desire wrapped around her.

This is what she wanted, what she had been missing without even knowing it. She anticipated his movements, rolling her body against his. Closing her eyes, she let herself get lost in the music and Sean.

They moved together, blending perfectly into each other. She turned in his arms, laying her head on his chest and listening to him hum along to the song. The aching points of her nipples pressed against him, and she stroked down his arms. Here, in the darkness behind her eyelids, she could pretend they were alone in some perfect place where time had no meaning.

He stroked over her back in a light touch that sent tingles through her. Emboldened, she pressed her hips to his and let him dip her back, the hard bulge of his erection pressing against her. When one of his large hands gripped her thigh, she willingly let him slide it over his hip so that his cock pressed against her wet pussy. His groan blended into the music as she rocked against him.

More. She wanted more of this pleasure that chased the darkness from her soul, and brought sunlit warmth to the icy prison around her heart. Threading her fingers through his hair was pure decadence. The warm strands felt like silk beneath her hands. They continued to rock together, to follow the beats of the music and each other. The feeling of his cock pressing against her swollen clit had her gasping, and his growling response shot through her like a drink of strong tequila.

He woke her sensual side, coaxed it to burning life with his body and music. Her eyes almost opened as he lifted her other leg so both her legs were wrapped around his waist with his big hands cupping her bottom. So strong, he held her as if she were nothing, as if he could hold her for hours and wouldn't tire. Running her hands through his hair, she lifted her face to his in a silent invitation.

Some strange language rolled off his tongue before he closed the distance between them. The moment their lips touched, her world came undone. A wild pleasure roared through her, and she ground herself against him as she moaned into his exquisite kiss. He tasted like the ocean, clean with a slight hint of salt and cold wind. Lips firm yet soft brushed against hers and sent sparks of pure lust straight to her throbbing pussy

Pulling him closer, she rocked her hips against his, their lips mimicking the movements of their bodies. He was impossibly hard between her legs, and big. Each thrust had her slit running the length of his cock until she was making little pleading noises against his lips every time he ground into her clit. She couldn't remember the last time she'd had an orgasm, or even wanted one. Her body was starving for release.

He licked at the seam of her lips, and she eagerly opened for him, sighing into his mouth at the first stroke of his tongue. His kiss was just like the rest of him, made for her. His hands moved lower, curving beneath her bottom and changing the angle of her hips so that he hit her clit dead-on with every thrust of his hips. The seam of her pants were soaked with her desire, and she wondered if he could feel it. She could certainly smell her musk as he teased her body into an even higher state of arousal.

The world narrowed down to him rocking between her legs and his lips against her mouth. Closer now, her body tensed against his with her orgasm just out of reach. Never in her life had she been this out of control with desire, but she didn't care. This was right and so very good.

The ache in her body increased until it bordered on pain and Sean seemed to sense that. He broke his kiss and trailed his lips down her neck, placing little bites that had her shuddering against him. Just a little bit more and she would be there, bursting with pleasure like an over-ripe peach.

Arching back, she sighed and rolled her hips into him in a move that had him stumbling as his cock jerked between her legs. A cold sensation brushed against her just before the door to the practice room banged open and a high-pitched female voice yelled, "Carmella, what the hell are you doing?"

A bucket of icy sewage couldn't have had more of an effect on her than that voice. Dropping her legs from around Sean's waist, she stared in horror at the sight of Dianta and three of her pet instructors glaring at her from the doorway. Dianta wore a bright pink miniskirt coupled with an almost transparent white top. It was obvious she wasn't wearing a bra beneath.

"I—" The words choked off in her throat as shame and humiliation came crashing down on her soul, killing her joy and desire.

"How dare you act in such a manner at my school?" Dianta said in disgust. "Sean, I'm so sorry she threw herself at you like this."

Sean pushed her behind him so he stood between her and Dianta. "She didn't throw herself at me. I—"

"Your father would have been ashamed to see you acting like this," one of Dianta's pet instructors said in Portuguese so Sean wouldn't understand. "Acting like a whore where anyone could walk in on you. I'm glad it was us and not some of our innocent young students that had to see you grinding yourself on him like slut. He looks so humiliated to have been caught with you."

Shame slammed into Carmella, and she pushed away from Sean. She couldn't look at his face, couldn't see the embarrassment there. They were right; she was acting like a woman with no morals. He must think she did this with everyone. She dodged his hand and slunk past him. The coldness that accompanied Dianta's arrival crushed the warmth that he had given her, ate it up and left her shivering.

She was no one, nothing, and would never be good enough for Sean.

His yells to come back fell on deaf ears, and she ran down the hallway with tears streaming down her face.

****

Working under the harsh glare of the florescent lights, Carmella stood back from the dress dummy and evaluated the headdress of the Snow Queen costume. Small white feathers fastened to a glittering white cap that would be secured to the head with bobby pins. Most of the glitter and the neon blue rhinestones were glued on the cap itself. A carefully spread series of plumes made the crown of the piece.

The headdress had to be worn for hours at a time. If it was too heavy, it could injure the wearer. Not that she would mind if Dianta's head popped off, but it might scare the children. Her lips curved in a humorless grin as she glued another rhinestone to the base of a feather.

It was a wonder she'd gotten any work done. Over and over her mind replayed her time with Sean as she tried to resolve what she was feeling. One moment she would be filled with a bright joy that made her glow with happiness, and the next, cold ice would kill off the warm happiness and leave her bleak and shivering. It felt as if her mind was at war against itself, and her body paid the price. She ached deep in her bones, and her heart actually hurt.

Every time she thought of Sean, a vicious headache would begin behind her eyes, and she would have to sit and breathe until it passed. As long as she didn't think about him and all of the carnal pleasures that she wanted to sample with him, her head was fine. But one thought about the strength of his shoulders or the way his hair had felt beneath her fingers had that sharp agony back with a vengeance. She was so confused and tired of being cold.

Different ways to sabotage Dianta's costume seemed to be the only thing she could safely consider. Not that she actually would—she was too big of a believer in karma—but it was nice to imagine the peroxide blonde falling off the float and into a convenient pile of dog poop. Her blood still boiled after the revelation about Dianta being responsible for her being a seamstress and the way she treated her in front of Sean today. What was wrong with her? Why didn't she stand up for herself and stop letting Dianta push her around? It was as if her self-respect had died the day Miguel inherited the samba school.

High heels clicked, and cheap perfume filled the air. *Speak of the devil*, Carmella thought as she checked her watch. Odd, Dianta was usually long gone from the samba school by now. Maybe she was back to yell at her again. Dianta had made it clear that if she ever caught Carmella so much as looking at Sean she would be fired. A row of blue and green drummers' costumes swayed as Dianta shoved the rack to the side.

Carmella froze with the needle in her hand. Behind Dianta stood Branco, gripping his black wooden cane in his gloved hands. Scars ran down the side of one cheek and disappeared into the collar of his dress shirt. Though he was past middle age, his body was still strong beneath his expensive black suit. His dark eyes locked with hers as he said, "*O sono agora e esquece.*"

****

Branco watched as Dianta brushed past Carmella's frozen form, making little cooing sounds as she admired the headdress. "Are you sure she can't hear us, *meu amor*?" Dianta asked as she held up the top of her costume.

"Not unless I want her to. She's in Guaricana's power now. The spell makes her as helpless as a bug trapped in amber." Branco watched Dianta with a dead smile.

"In that case..." Dianta purred, and she slid to Branco, running her hands over his dusky cheeks and kissing him as though his throat held the secrets of the universe.

Carmella remained frozen, the rise and fall of her chest and the occasional blink the only disruption of her still state. Her mind slept, and she remained unaware of everything around her.

Branco traced a gloved hand down Dianta's cheek. "You were wise to call me. My spell should have been strong enough to kill any attraction to a man, to squash any self-esteem that would allow her to think he might like her back. We need her to remain a virgin."

"You should have seen her with that DJ. They were all, but fucking in the middle of the room. Thankfully I managed to break them up before anything happened. I thought we didn't have to worry about her when she started dressing like a boy. The only man she has had for company is that fag, Tian."

Giving Dianta's butt a pat, Branco turned and looked at Carmella. "Be careful of Sean Kalmus. He is...a special favorite of his god. Much like I'm a special favorite of Guaricana. I can't be here on the days Sean visits. Only call me when you are sure he's not coming."

Dianta gave him a disbelieving stare. "What can a stupid DJ do to you? You're a voodoo master, a High Priest of Guaricana. You have spilled oceans of blood for his glory."

"It is best to strike from the dark, Dianta. To be the knife in the back. A betrayer. You should know this better than anyone," Branco replied lightly.

Dianta's face twisted into an ugly snarl that no amount of plastic surgery could make pretty. "I told that little bitch," she said and pointed at Carmella, "she would rue the day she stole the samba crown from me."

"Yes, my dear. Now you have her business, her family is destroyed, and she's a broken seamstress making your clothes. You were well rewarded for bringing her to us. Guaricana enjoys using a favorite of a god of Creation for his bait."

Slightly appeased, Dianta let out a huff. "When she's no longer of use to us, what are you going to do with her? Can I have her?" Malice glittered in her eyes.

"I'm afraid not. I have a better plan for her." Using the edge of his cane, Branco lifted a lock of Carmella's long hair and let it fall. "Why, our little Carmella is going to be famous. She's going to take the blame for us in a spectacular fashion." Branco flicked through a rack of costumes and checked to make sure they were still alone. "The death count is starting to get too high. The papers are calling on the police to do something about whoever is whipping all these young men to death."

Dianta snorted. "As if Guaricana would ever let them harm us."

Branco gave her a humorless smile. "We need just a few more men to complete our spell." He stroked a hand over Dianta's face and whispered, "Immortality."

A shudder ripped through Dianta's pin-up body. "Then we must be careful and keep her pure for a little while longer." She kissed his hand. "If we play our cards right, we could be famous. We could do tours of the samba school where the murderess planned her killings."

Branco held his hands out. "All of those poor men found whipped to death in the alleys will be her victims. The press will have a field day with it. And Guaricana will make sure there is never a question of her guilt. After all, she's the last person all these men have been seen with. The mysterious woman in the red dress."

Dianta laughed and clapped her hands. "Perfect. We should have her start targeting wealthy tourists. The police don't give much of a rat's ass if the low-class locals disappear, but if we tell her to feed on only wealthy foreign tourists...well, they'll step up their efforts to find her."

Strutting around Carmella, Dianta stuck her tongue out at her in a childish display of temper. "I had better start planning what outfit to wear when the news breaks." She gave a theatrical sigh and clasped her hands together. "Such a tragedy. I knew something was wrong with our frumpy little seamstress, but I had no idea she was the biggest serial killer in the history of Brazil."

Branco nodded and stepped toward Carmella. "I will strengthen the spell. It will remind her how worthless she is, how undeserving of attention and love. She'll avoid that DJ like the plague. Tomorrow night, we will send the succubus out again to hunt. Perhaps for the last time."

Dianta sat down in the frayed lawn chair with a pretty pout, batting her fake eyelashes at Branco. "It would be so much easier if we could use a non-virgin."

"Yes, but Guaricana's succubus can only take over a virgin's body. We need to keep her chaste until we are done with her." Branco looked into Carmella's vacant amber eyes and began to chant softly.

Chapter Five

Head slumped against the glass, Carmella stared out the dirty window of the bus. People occupied every space, and she was lucky to have snagged a seat. Next to her, an older woman clutched her cheap purse and scanned everyone on the bus with suspicion. Identifying the greatest threat to her handbag, she narrowed her gaze at a young boy dressed in dirty clothes with greasy hair. The boy stared back at her, his face older than his years as he gave her a sullen look and a sneer. They continued to measure each other. He looked away first and cleaned his dirty nails with a pocketknife.

Turning away from the silent display of bus dominance, Carmella examined the passing buildings while she thought about her day. Most of it had been spent hiding from Sean's choreographers, Monica and Whitney. They were stunning, tall women who dressed with style and moved with a self-assured grace. She couldn't stand to be around them, to be reminded of her inadequacies. It would be like placing a lump of clay next to a blown-glass vase. No, a lump of manure.

Fatima stopped by to let her know Monica was looking for her, but Carmella pleaded a massive headache and asked Fatima to cover for her. She couldn't face them. They were amazing, world-famous dancers, and she was a washed-up seamstress. It was cruel of Sean to send them to speak with her. So she hid in the bathroom or behind her racks of costumes when she heard their voices. She felt like a coward, but the thought of having to perform for them made her sick to the point of dry heaving.

Didn't he see yesterday how clumsy she was, how her dancing was amateurish at best? She could still remember the look of disgust on Sean's face as she tried to teach him how to dance, how he'd recoiled from her touch. For a moment, another memory surfaced—the feeling of his lips crushed against hers as they swayed together in perfect rhythm. A sharp burst of cold pain in her head accompanied that image, and she pressed her fingers to her temples in an effort to alleviate the ache. Once the pain faded she couldn't remember what she had been thinking.

Sean's face and his slate-colored eyes kept on popping up in her thoughts. A brief surge of happiness filled her, quickly replaced by shame and embarrassment. He'd been so kind to say those nice lies to her. He must have felt sorry for her when he saw her pathetic attempt at belly dancing and wanted to make her feel better. Sean was out of her league; so far above her that she couldn't even see him.

Briefly, she stroked a hand over her pocket. In it was a stolen CD liner from Fatima's DJ Kal CD, and it had Sean's picture on the back. At least she had this to remember him by. In a week, he would be long gone, having moved on to whatever adventures and beautiful women his life must be filled with. And she would still be Carmella, seamstress and Dianta's whipping post. It was all that she could ever hope for.

The jerk of the bus knocked her out of her depressing thoughts. A green-painted grocery store with its graffiti-stained walls signaled her stop. Moving past the sullen woman who clutched her purse and gave Carmella a glare, she shoved her way through the mass of bodies. The air outside the bus was a relief, even if it was thick and muggy. Not everyone used—or could afford—deodorant on the crowded bus.

Head down, backpack clutched to her shoulders with both hands, she hustled as fast as she could down the sidewalk to her apartment. The pavement in the distance shimmered beneath waves of heat in the baking sun. Spring was just beginning in this part of the world, but it already felt like the dead of summer.

The long, navy shirt she wore clung to her back with sweat. Cars zoomed past her with their expensive stereos blasting, the sound system often costing more than the decrepit vehicle itself. A couple of children in threadbare clothes ran by, and she had to spin to dodge them on the broken concrete of the sidewalk.

Still hunched tight, she opened the iron gate to her apartment complex and blew out a grateful sigh. No one had tried to mug her, rape her, or sell her drugs on the way home. Maybe things were looking up.

The smile quickly died on her lips as she saw the local pimp, Ramon, waiting for her in the doorway. He pitched the brown cigarette he was smoking into the struggling bushes and gave her a big smile. Gold teeth twinkled in the fading early evening light, and the pockmarks in his tan skin stood out in sharp relief. He flicked the collar of his black satin shirt and gave her a wink. "Carmella," he purred at her. "Why do you hide that lovely body underneath those clothes?"

The gate key still in her hand, Carmella remained frozen like a mouse in front of a snake. Ramon had been trying to get Carmella to whore for him since she moved in. So far she had managed to avoid him, but it her luck had run out.

Pulling up her shoulders, she tried to appear tough and unafraid. As she climbed the concrete steps to the foyer, Ramon moved so he was right next to her. Pressing his groin against her hip, he pushed her into the metal railing of the stairs. She bit her lip so hard she tasted blood.

"Aye, *senhora bonita*. Why do you always run away from me? I can make you lots of money. You won't even have to work the streets. As pretty as you are, I'll put you in my strip club." Ramon spoke into her ear, the smell of his cheap cologne and stale coffee washing over her.

"Piss off, Ramon. I'm not for sale," Carmella replied, hoping he didn't hear the tremor in her voice.

Ramon pressed against her harder, grinding his erection into her side. "Everyone is for sale. Even you, Carmella." He said her name with an exaggerated roll on the *R* that sprayed spittle on the side of her face. "You want to live in this dump forever? I can take you out of here, baby. I can take care of you."

Using her backpack, Carmella managed to shove him back a step. "I've seen how you take care of your women. I've seen them walking down the hall with black eyes or split lips. I. Am. Not. For. Sale." She emphasized each word with a jab of her backpack into his stomach.

Lifting his lip in a snarl, Ramon grabbed her arm in a bruising hold. "You think you're better than us? You think you're somebody special? You're nothing, you're no one, and you're just another worthless bitch. Look at you! My lowest whore has more respect for herself."

The words struck a blow to her already wounded ego. He said everything she felt about herself, everything she'd thought when she looked in the mirror this morning. Thrown off guard, all she could do was stare at him with tears in her eyes.

Ramon smoothed his hair back with a hand covered in gold rings and gave her an oily smile. "Come with me, baby. I'll make those tears go away. A couple lines of coke and you won't hurt anymore."

Carmella felt her lip curl in disgust. "I'd rather spend the rest of my life cleaning toilets than *ever* let you touch me. You disgust me. A real man doesn't have to beat women and pay for his sex."

"You *cadela estúpida*!" Ramon growled a second before he slapped her face. Her eyes watered from the pain, and she lifted a hand to her wounded cheek. No blood, but her cheekbone throbbed.

Carmella stood there for a moment, stunned, before she backhanded Ramon across the face with all her strength. Ramon sailed across the concrete steps, landing at the bottom with a thud. She didn't know who was more surprised at her unusual strength, her or the man looking up at her now with murder in his eyes. The right arm of his shirt had torn during his fall, and his skinned elbow dripped blood down his hand. His tongue worried his lip, and he spat blood onto the steps at her feet.

"Oh, you bitch. You're going to pay," he crooned as he slipped a butterfly knife out of his pocket. Staggering to his feet, he wiped the blood from his split lip and began to lumber toward her.

Terrified, Carmella backed up the steps, not taking her eyes off him. How had she managed to hit him as hard as she did? He outweighed her by at least eighty pounds. No way she could have knocked him down the steps with one blow. Those thoughts were secondary to the fear coursing through her, bright and silver-hot.

The door squeaked open behind her, and a large dog began to bark and snarl. "Get out of here, Ramon," a stern woman's voice yelled over the loud barks. "I told you not to step foot on my property again. I let your whores stay here because I pray to the Blessed Virgin they will find the strength to leave you. But if they keep letting you in here, I will kick them out."

Turning around, Carmella looked gratefully to her guardian angels. It was Mrs. Amável, the landlady. The furry guardian angel with the deep bark was Mrs. Amavel's chief of security, Gabriel. Standing as high as Carmella's hip, Gabriel was a 115-pound German Rottweiler. Normally as sweet as a lamb to Carmella, right now he was snapping and snarling at Ramon like a crazed beast.

The tip of Ramon's knife pointed at Carmella, glinting orange and gold in the light of the setting sun. "This isn't done. No bitch hits me and gets away with it."

Mrs. Amável loosed the leash holding Gabriel back, and the dog lunged down a few steps at Ramon. Turning white, Ramon backed away quickly and ran out the gate.

Carmella let out a shuddering breath and sat down hard on the concrete step. "I'm so sorry, Mrs. Amável. I didn't mean to bring trouble to your apartments."

With a sniff, Mrs. Amável said, "Don't worry about it. That one has been a thorn in my side since I bought this place. Gods forgive me, but I keep hoping he will get arrested or killed one of these days."

Gabriel came over to Carmella and gave her a big, stinky dog kiss on the side of her face. Laughing, Carmella hugged him close and buried her face in his soft neck. "Next payday I owe you a big bone from the butcher, Gabriel." He gave her a big doggy smile and another lick.

"He's a good boy," Mrs. Amável agreed. Carmella took a deep breath and walked into the cool air of the foyer with Mrs. Amável. "I'm afraid you've made an enemy with Ramon. He's the kind of filth that will take any opportunity to come after you."

They stopped in front of the door to Mrs. Amavel's first-floor apartment. The white tiles of the floor were missing some grout, but it was clean. Mrs. Amável only let women rent apartments in the building, and there was always a high demand for her units. Safety was hard to find in the ghetto, and the fathers and brothers of the women staying here often kept an eye on the place.

"I know," Carmella said in a tired voice. "I just don't know what I can do about it. Other than get a gun. And with the way the justice system works around here, I'd probably be the one in jail if I shot him."

Mrs. Amável gave her a sympathetic pat on the shoulder. "Why don't you have your friends with the limo take care of him?"

"My what?" Carmella asked in confusion as she shifted her backpack.

"Your friends with the limo. You know, they pick you up in the evenings a couple times a week. I see you go out the front door and meet them. Always in a tight red dress." Mistaking Carmella's stunned silence for censure, Mrs. Amável continued, "Mind you, I'm not spying, of course. It's just that a limo attracts attention in this neighborhood. And I'm not used to seeing you all dressed up with all that makeup."

"You must have me confused with someone else. I stay in my apartment at night. I can't remember the last time I went out, and I haven't been in a limo since my *quinceañera*," Carmella protested as bile rose in her throat.

Mrs. Amável paused and studied her face. "Oh, I must have been mistaken then. You don't look well. Are you all right?" At her feet, Gabriel began to whine and lick Carmella's hand.

"No, I'm not feeling so well. I have to go." Carmella stumbled back and climbed the stairs to her apartment.

From below, Mrs. Amável yelled, "I hope you feel better. Drink some tea and make sure your door is locked tonight. I don't want anything to happen to you because of that cockroach Ramon."

Carmella raised a hand in response, her stomach sloshing and churning with acid.

An hour later, she lay on her back in her bed, staring at the ceiling as the fan spun the humid air. What in the world was Mrs. Amável talking about? She stayed in her apartment all night, and she never had any visitors, let alone a limo come for her. Could she have mistaken her for someone else? It was possible, but the walkway and the front entrance were well lit by bright sodium security lights. Maybe there was another woman living here with long dark hair and a similar build. It wouldn't be beyond the realm of reason in Brazil.

The mention of the red dress was the part that made her heart skip a beat in fear. It had to be just a coincidence the woman Mrs. Amável saw wore a dress the same color as the one she always wore in her nightmares. She didn't even own any red dresses. After the third time she had that nightmare she had checked her closet. Nope, no red dress or six-inch black heels. At the time, she had laughed off her own foolishness...now she wasn't so sure.

Pressing the heels of her palms into her eyes, she prayed in desperation. *Please, help me. I don't know what is going on, but I'm afraid I'm losing my mind. Please, someone, please help me.*

There was no answer, and she felt exhaustion drag her down into sleep. The gentle breeze of the fan moved the air over her face, and her quilt from home held her softly. Her last thoughts before drifting off were of

Sean and running her fingers through his fine red hair.

****

Two hours later, Carmella's amber eyes snapped open with a flash as the succubus took over. She sat straight up in bed and groaned, running her hands down her body in an indulgent caress. Arching her back like a cat, she stroked her fingertips over her chest and into her hair, a laughing purr coming from her lips. With a roll of her hips any stripper would envy, she sauntered across the room into the kitchen where she turned on the lights.

Moving a chair over from the tiny breakfast table, she stood on it and lifted a ceiling panel over. A bundle of red fabric wrapped around something came out of the crawlspace, and she set it on the table. Licking her lips, the succubus shook out the red dress and placed the shiny-black heels and makeup off to the side.

After a quick change, and a heavy application of makeup, Carmella picked up the phone and quickly called Branco.

"I'm here. Any special instructions?" she asked, her voice a husky rasp that brought to mind illicit pleasures done in the dark. Her arched eyebrows rose as she listened to Branco's directions. "A foreigner...with money? Hmmm, yes, that would be a fun diversion. I know just the place too. I always have good hunting there. It's packed with desperate tourists looking for some action. And most of them still have a tan line from the wedding ring they've shoved in their pocket. Such a delicious feast of shame and guilt, enough to glut myself on as I fuck them to death."

Branco's voice deepened with anger. "You will do nothing to risk Carmella's virginity."

Anger crashed through the succubus as Branco's order bound her to his will. "I know our agreement, summoner. I will not complete the seduction."

"Soon you'll be able to feast. We are almost finished with little Carmella and once we have what we need you can use her body however you wish, as long as it ends with her taking the blame for all the deaths. You will make sure that her guilt is guaranteed."

The snarl faded, and in its place anticipation bordering on greed lit her eyes as her fingers stroked the phone cord. "I'll be sad to see this body go, but it will be so much fun to lose its virginity. Poor girl, she won't know what hit her when she wakes up in a pile of corpses, all men she brought to be killed. I think I'll leave one alive long enough to rape her then leave them both as soon as I'm forced out. Let's make tonight count then. I'll be waiting for the limo. Good-bye."

She reached down and straightened the line of her thong. With a final glance in the mirror to check her makeup, she smiled at herself and turned out the lights. Finally she was going to be able to feed, and she intended to gorge herself on the soul of a sinner.

Chapter Six

Blood red and pumpkin orange lights throbbed across the dance floor of the packed club. Two stories of patrons looked down on Sean as he neared the end of his set, his shirt long gone, sweat covering his muscled chest and shining in the lights. Behind him, Kell kept an eye on the crowd, constantly scanning for any signs of trouble. Off to his right side, their dancers performed a high-stepping Irish jig to the music in short, black metallic dresses and sparkling green tights. Sean's music note tattoo was embroidered on the back of each dress, an extra blessing for his dancers that gave them power and stamina from his music.

Each of his sets was different. During a full show, he would mix traditional Irish songs with melodies from Europe, Asia, Africa, and South America. Every song brought its own special brand of magic. It didn't translate well onto the CDs or DVDs, but during a live show he could enchant an audience and move their souls with his music.

Sean let the melody flow over him, loving the magic of its beat moving through the crowd. He was feeding their joy, their hope. The music reshaped their hearts to be fertile soil for kindness. This was part of his gift, part of the magic he'd received from his god Maponus as one of his Chosen hands on Earth. The only thing that kept him from fully immersing himself into the music was the thought of Carmella.

Monica and Whitney had tried to find her at the samba school, but she was nowhere around. They talked with a friend of hers, a man named Tian. He told them about Carmella's father and mother and the rough time she had been having lately. When Sean heard about the series of tragedies she'd endured, he couldn't help but think right away that someone had cursed her. That would explain the touch of darkness that he'd felt in her and her resistance to the natural bonding between their souls.

He kept praying she would come to his show tonight. She must have felt the same connection he did. It was in her gaze when she looked at him, her eyes sable-brown with flecks of sweet honey. Her dark hair set off the golden tone of her soft skin, and her body had the most amazing elegance. The sunlight embraced her and turned her into a living piece of art when she danced.

The song began to wind down, the high flutes standing out and independent of the cello as he pulled the low synthetic harmony away. His skin seemed to burn with energy, and a familiar aura made him eagerly search the crowd of moving bodies. There it was. That brush of her energy that rang in his soul like bells.

He turned his head to the side and mouthed, "Carmella", to Kell, who shook his head and rolled his eyes. Rocking back on his heels, he tried to contain his excitement. He felt like a teenager on a first date with the girl of his dreams.

A hint of discord came from the area where she stood and he tensed. Reaching out with his energy, he gently brushed against her soul and got that impression of something being wrong again. Maybe she was sick, and that was why she couldn't be found at the school today. While he'd like to believe that a simple illness kept her away, he couldn't help but worry that it was something more. His interactions with her had been quite public and it was possible that whoever had cursed her was aware of his interest and that put her in danger. He vowed that tonight he would find a way to save her, to convince her to trust him enough to come home with him.

Searching the dance floor, Sean scanned the crowd until he found her again. She wore a tight red dress that was built for sin. One slender arm curved around the shoulders of an older, sunburned man in a salmon-pink shirt. She appeared to be laughing at whatever he was saying, smiling at him as he moved his hand down her back and over the plush curve of her butt.

With clenched teeth, Sean bit back an oath. What the hell was going on? Was that fat old man her boyfriend? Was she his mistress? He barely remembered to finish the song, waiting a couple beats too long. His dancers turned to give him a worried look, but he mustered a smile and bowed to the audience as the applause rolled over him.

Grabbing a towel and a bottle of water, he stalked to the back of the stage by Kell. "Carmella is here, but she's letting some fat man grab her ass like he owns it," Sean shouted over the music from the club DJ beginning his set. He wiped the sweat from his face and chugged the water, trying to get a hold of the anger and hurt.

"What? Are you sure? She didn't seem like the type to do something like that." Kell frowned as he tried to spot Carmella among the flashing lights and writhing bodies.

Sean took a deep breath as his dancers filed past. He nodded and thanked them with a forced smile, trying to keep everything as normal as possible. Craning his head, he found her in the crowd again, still rubbing herself against the fat man and twining her slender fingers in his thinning hair. She didn't even glance Sean's way, and he wondered if she even knew he was here. Was she trying to play some kind of game to make him jealous? His stomach clenched as he had a terrible thought, something even worse than watching a sweaty bastard grope his harmony.

Half closing his eyes, he opened his mind and looked at the auras in the crowd. It was like shifting his vision to look at something far away and then up close. He scanned the crowd again, trying to find her familiar violet glow. His teeth snapped with an audible click, and he grabbed for a sword on his back that wasn't there. Now that he was looking for it, the answer as to what was wrong with Carmella was as clear as an oil slick on water. Rage filled him at the thought of someone, or something, harming his harmony.

Kell grasped his shoulder, holding Sean back as he tried to leap into the crowd. "What's going on, Sean?"

Not taking his eyes off Carmella simpering and tracing her fingers over the rotund man's sweaty face, Sean spat out, "Something is using her body. I can see bits of purple shining through, so she's still there, but her body is possessed."

Kell swore in a long, low breath. "Any idea what it is?" He tried to see over the crowd.

Sean shook his head. "I'm not familiar with the psychic scent. It smells like...cheap perfume...and decay...and guilt, if guilt had a scent."

"Succubus," Kell replied simply.
"What?"

"Succubus, cheap perfume, decay, guilt. That's a succubus." Catching Sean's incredulous expression, Kell said in a defensive tone, "Don't look at me like that. I've never slept with one of them. I'd sooner stick my dick in an electrical socket than fuck with a succubus. They prey on married men, the better your marriage, the more they want you to break your vow of fidelity. That's what they feed on, the guilt of your sin. I read about it in my *Demonologists Today* magazine."

"And here I thought the only thing you read in the bathroom were dirty magazines." Sean grinned and then sobered as Carmella tipped her head back to allow the fat man access to her neck with his thick tongue. "We need to get her out of this club and back to the hotel. I can get the spirit out of her, but we're going to need to get her to contact whatever god she's a favorite of and ask for his or her help."

Kell nodded and spoke into his cell phone, asking the limo driver to pull around back and wait for them.

Sean cracked his knuckles. "Then we are going to find out who did this to my harmony and make them pay."

"I'll go get her. As much as I love my wife, I have to be like crack to a succubus." Kell gave a too-innocent look. "If she throws herself on me, you can tell Mary it wasn't my fault. I was just taking one for the team."

Sean gave him a narrow-eyed glare. "Keep your hands to yourself if you like them attached to your body. I'll be out back in the limo. If the succubus within her catches a glimpse of me, she's going to run."

Nodding to the bouncers keeping the crowd of fans away from the stage, Sean toweled himself down and prepared for a fight.

****

Smooth, deep voice... like fine cognac... rolling over her soul. The world around her rocked with motion, and the arms carrying her tightened their grip. Carmella tried to open her eyes, but they wouldn't obey. Her heart raced as she panicked, mind fighting through the darkness, smothering it into sleep. The man's voice interrupted her terror, melted it away. There was nothing but his song, an unfamiliar melody that relaxed her like a thousand warm baths. It was better to sleep now. She was safe, she was warm, and the man singing to her would protect her.

Deep voices tugged at her conscious mind, dragging her up from the comfortable darkness of sleep. An unfamiliar green patterned bedspread came into focus then the side of a polished wood table that wasn't hers. Lifting herself from the soft bed, disoriented, she found herself looking into Sean's face as he sat in a chair next to the bed.

"Sean, I missed you," she murmured as she put her head back down on the pillow. It was good that Sean was here; he would watch over her while she slept.

Wait, what was Sean doing here?

Sitting straight up, she clutched her hands over her chest. He watched her with a careful expression on his handsome face. They appeared to be in some kind of plush bedroom. A vase of fresh orchids stood on the small table before the window. Expensive prints hung on the walls, and thick brocade curtains flanked the sparkling lights of Rio, but the large screen TV was bolted to the dresser. The small room service menu next to the phone confirmed that she was in a hotel room.

A hint of red caught her attention, and she looked down to see the red dress from her nightmares covering her body. With a piercing scream, she leaped out of bed and tried to tear it off. He was up in an instant, holding her arms against her sides as she fought to pull the dress off. "Let me go! I have to get this off! What is going on?" Carmella screamed into his face.

He held her easily in his grip. The smell of his clean shirt was comforting, as was the soft, magical tune he hummed. She stopped fighting for a moment and started to shake. Terror and confusion battled with delight at being held in his arms.

"Kell, grab a T-shirt and a pair of my jogging shorts from the dresser," Sean yelled into the sitting room of the suite.

"Got it," came a rough voice from the other side.

"Carmella, please listen to me. You have to hear what I'm saying. Are you with me? Do you want a drink?" Sean asked in a gentle voice.

The way he softened his tone and crooned out the words rubbed against her skin like fur. If this situation weren't so absurd, she would have been giggling behind her hands at the idea of a furry voice.

"Yes," she managed to stutter out through chattering teeth.

"Yes you're with me, or yes you want a drink?"

"Yes to both. Sean, what is going on?"

"I'll explain everything in a minute. I know this sounds utterly bizarre, but please trust me. I will do everything in my power to keep you safe."

The conviction in his voice helped quiet the panic swirling through her mind.

Closing her eyes, she leaned her forehead against his chest. Barely coming to his shoulders, she was grateful for his size. It seemed like nothing could touch her when he was near. Almost against her will, she relaxed against his warmth as he hummed and ran his hand down her hair. This felt so familiar, being held in his arms and losing herself in his touch. She tried to grasp at the memory, but it kept just out of reach.

A throat clearing loudly made her try to pull away from Sean and she opened her eyes. He held her tight and turned them both to face the doorway. The shaggy man stood there with some clothes in his hand and an uncomfortable expression on his bearded face. Her mind dreamily noted his name must be Kell. Come to think of it, all of her thinking was dreamy and unconcerned. She must be in shock, and if she was, she didn't want to come out of it. Not thinking was really relaxing.

"Toss it on the bed, Kell. We'll be out in a second," Sean said against the top of her head.

She closed her eyes again and tried to focus on his heartbeat. She didn't want to see anything right now, especially that hideous flash of red covering her body. Living in this perfect moment of not thinking sounded wonderful. Moving slowly, he lifted the weight of her hair off her back with his hand and ran it through his fingers.

Unfortunately, the more she tried not to think about the dress, the more she could feel it, and the more she wanted to tear it off. Moving gently, she stepped out of his arms and plucked at the smooth material with distaste. He watched her carefully, and the hint of desire in his gaze was too much to deal with on top of everything else. Looking at her feet seemed like the safest place at the moment. "Um, I need to use the bathroom to change."

"I can't leave you alone right now, Carmella. The situation is...complicated." He ran his hands through his auburn hair, and she watched the muscles of his biceps flex in his arm. "I have to ask for you to trust me again. I'll turn my back, but I have to stay with you."

Cheeks flaming, Carmella averted her gaze and grabbed the clothes. A quick peek showed his back as he faced the dark windows. Working as swiftly as possible, she stripped off the dress with a snarl of revulsion. A shocked gasp escaped her as she looked down at her underwear. What the hell was she doing in a black lace thong?

Sean spun around when she gasped, and his jaw dropped open while his broad chest filled as he took a deep breath. Erotic electricity crackled through the air, and his gaze on her body actually felt like fingers brushing against her skin.

With a very girly "Eeep!", she turned her back so he wouldn't see her breasts. His energy brushed over her skin like a physical caress that started at her shoulders and worked its way down to her rear end. Her thong clad rear end. With another squeak she tried to cover her butt with her hands as those phantom fingers trailed across her cheeks, making goose bumps rise along her skin.

Sean coughed loudly and said in a strained voice, "Sorry. I thought you were in trouble. Uh, sorry about my aura. Got away from me again."

"Nope, fine," Carmella peeped. Yep, just woke up in a dress from a nightmare, in a thousand-dollar-a-night suite, with the world famous DJ Kal getting a good look at her butt while he lost control of something he called his aura. Totally normal night. A hysterical giggle bubbled in her throat. Clearing her throat to choke back the giggle, Carmella said, "Okay, I'm dressed."

His blue eyes darkened to a deep gray as he looked slowly over her. She felt exposed, her body flushed and sensitive. His gaze lingered on her hips for a moment before moving to her breasts. In a delicious mixture of arousal and embarrassment, she felt her nipples tighten to points beneath the thin t-shirt. Sean's nostrils flared, and he sucked in a quick breath, taking a half step forward before turning around.

"Come into the living room. I'll get you a drink and try to explain what you're doing here," Sean said in a rough voice. Even now his speech seemed to have a melody to it.

"Okay," Carmella answered faintly. He could have invited her to skydive naked over a patch of cacti, and she would have agreed with a happy smile.

Before following Sean into the next room, Carmella paused for a moment and glared at the red dress lying on the floor. Taking in a deep breath, she spat on it and kicked it across the room. Scared, angry, confused, though slightly aroused, Carmella felt more alive than she had in months.

Chapter Seven

The chink of ice hitting glass led Carmella into the next room through the French doors. Sean knelt in front of a stainless steel mini-fridge, raiding the tiny bottles of alcohol. A sofa, table, and two chairs were shoved against the wall, and a rolled-up oriental carpet sat in the corner.

Kell hunched over his laptop and slammed away on the keys as his eyes darted over the screen.

Clearing her throat, Carmella said, "I'll take tequila if they have it."

"How is Cabo Wabo?" Sean asked, holding up a tiny bottle of amber liquid.

Their hands brushed as Carmella took the little bottle from him, and a rush of electricity brushed against her. Her nipples tightened into hard points and she tried to regain control over her hormones. In an effort to distract herself, she tried to focus on something other than Sean and she noticed the large box of salt sitting on the counter over the fridge.

"I don't know how they do tequila shots where you come from, but around here, we just use a pinch of salt."

"It's for something else," Kell replied from the other side of the room while staring at the computer screen.

"Let's take a seat on the sofa, and I'll try to explain what's going on." Sean took her hand and rubbed his thumb over her knuckles. It made little goose bumps break out over her arm, and she suppressed a sigh as they sat down at the sofa pushed against the window. Beyond the glass, the lights of downtown Rio blazed into the night and reflected off the waters of the Atlantic Ocean.

Kell gave Sean a nod as they took a seat, and Sean's face closed into an angry mask. Bewildered, she sipped her small bottle and welcomed the burn of good tequila. "Thank you for the drink and the clothes." She turned so she could see both men, and her voice hardened. "Now can you please tell me what the heck I'm doing in your hotel room?"

Sean placed his arm over the couch behind her, and she found herself leaning back so she could feel his warmth. No matter how bizarre this was, being next to him was as natural as breathing. That made her even more nervous, and she self-medicated with another sip from the bottle.

Kell glanced at her. "Long story short, you were possessed by the spirit of a succubus. Sean managed to put it to sleep with his music, but it's still within you. We've figured a way to get it out, I think...probably," he finished with a game smile and then clicked his mouse.

She stared at Kell and Sean cleared his throat and said, "I was trying to think of a gentler way to tell you, but what Kell said is pretty much it. You came to the club I was spinning at tonight, and you were trying to get a married man to leave with you."

She blinked at him then chugged the rest of her tequila in two big swallows as fear chilled her from within. "Bullshit."

Kell gave her a sympathetic look as Sean gently said, "No bullshit. We could take you back to the club and show you the security tapes of you kissing an old fat man, but we don't have time for that right now."

She gripped the small bottle so hard her knuckles turned white and her fingers hurt. "I'd think you were playing a joke on me, but I've been having nightmares about that red dress for weeks. I haven't told anyone about it. There is no way you could have known." A revolted shudder whipped through her body. "What did you mean by it's still within me, and what exactly is a succubus?"

Kell opened his mouth, and Sean gave him a look that clearly said, *don't help*. "A succubus is a minor demon that seduces married men and then eats their guilt over cheating on their wives. The better the marriage, the more guilt, the happier the succubus. They usually use their own forms to do this, but for some reason, this one is using your body." Sean took her hand in his, rubbing her knuckles with his thumb in a soothing manner.

"I'm pretty sure your succubus was attached to you with an entry charm," Kell added as he glanced up from the screen of his laptop. "We have to find the charm, put it in a salt circle, and destroy it with a blessed object. That will break the spirit's connection to you and contain it long enough to banish it."

"I've been sleeping with married men?" she said in a horrified whisper. "But I'm a virgin!"

Both men glanced at each other, and Kell shifted uncomfortably, then shrugged. "Might as well tell the lass."

"Okay, seriously, if you two don't stop giving each other looks and nods, I'm going to have to choke you both." She growled in frustration. "Tell me what?"

"Sorry, it umm...well, we didn't...you know, check or anything...but if you were a virgin before the succubus took you over, you're still one now. A succubus cannot force you to give up your virginity without losing your body as a vessel. And since you were still possessed at the club, and we haven't done anything to change your...state—I'd say it's safe to believe that you're still...intact." Sean's fair cheeks heated, and his eyes grew warm and dark.

"Oh," she said in a faint voice as she imagined Sean—checking her, those long fingers stroking her body like an instrument.

"Good, um...yeah." Her cheeks also flooded with heat as they stared at each other in the charged silence.

Kell snorted. "If you two are done blushing at each other like a couple of schoolgirls, we need to find that charm."

She considered giving Kell the finger. "What would it look like? Could it be clothing or jewelry or something like that?"

"Probably jewelry, you would have to wear it all the time."

She shook her head. "I don't wear any jewelry. You don't walk through my neighborhood wearing anything that might invite a mugging."

Looking confused, Sean held up her hand. "What about this ring?"

She stared at her hand then back at Sean. "What ring?"

"This ring, right here." He ran his finger over the knuckle by her middle finger.

Very carefully, as though she was speaking to a slow child, she said, "Sean, I'm not wearing a ring."

Kell frowned at her and said in an equally slow voice, "Yes, you are. Sean is touching it right now. It's a plain white circle, kind of looks like bone...er, ivory."

"No, I'm not wearing a ring." She jerked her hand away from Sean. "What's wrong with you guys? Don't you think I would know if I was wearing something on my hand?"

Sean took her hand and knocked it against her empty bottle on the table. It produced a chinking sound, like metal hitting glass. "Not if you've been put under a spell or hypnotized not to see it."

Beginning to cry, her voice shook as she said, "Son of a bitch." She rubbed away the tears before they could fall from her cheeks. "Can we please get this done? No more explanations. I just want it out of me."

"Yes." Sean stroked away a stray tear with his thumb. "I'm going to need you to stand in the middle of the room and follow my directions. I put the succubus to sleep at the club. She's in a state of limbo inside of you right now. We're going to wake the succubus up and draw her into the ring." Sean moved over to the counter above the fridge. "You should be able to see the ring and once the ring turns black, I want you to place it in the center of the circle of salt that I'm going to make."

She padded across the deep carpet and watched Sean spill the salt into a perfect white circle on the dark green carpet. Stroking her finger, she tried to feel the ring that they said was there. "Okay, what should I do?"

Kell spoke up from his laptop. "It might sting when you force the succubus out. You need to help Sean by not letting it deceive you. It will probably lie to you and try to manipulate you into letting it stay."

Placing his big hands on her shoulders, Sean gave her a gentle kiss on the forehead. Her whole body warmed from head to toe at the soft press of his lips. The kiss was both comforting and distracting.

"I swear I will not let anything hurt you, my harmony," he whispered against her forehead.

"Your harmony?"

Sean smiled and just gave her a wink. Once he was on the other side of the room, he grabbed a black case from behind the couch and set it on the table. Whistling a complicated tune, he pulled out a beautiful sword.

"Please tell me you're not going to use that on me," she said in what she hoped was a strong voice. Inside she shook like a scared Chihuahua.

Kell stood and handed Sean a simple silver flute. "No, we need a blessed instrument to destroy the ring. Sean just happens to have a sacred sword, blessed by the high priests and priestesses of over forty-eight different religions."

"Well, isn't that handy?" she said faintly as Sean sliced through the air with a simple twist of his wrist.

Handing the sword to Kell, Sean held the pipe to his lips. "Enough chitchat. Let's get this done before the sun rises."

Unsure what to do with herself, she crossed her arms and toyed with the sleeves of Sean's T-shirt as he began to play a simple melody on the pipe. No, it wasn't simple; it was complex ... riveting...beckoning. His slate-blue eyes watched her as he played, and she realized she was subconsciously swaying to the music with a roll of her hips.

Abruptly, she jerked as her finger began to hurt. It felt as though someone was slicing at the skin with a tiny knife. She looked in panic at Sean, but he just continued to play and watch her. Kell held a finger to his lips, motioning for her to be quiet. Gritting her teeth, she swallowed back a cry as the pain intensified. Her middle finger began to shiver and waver in her sight, like the heat rising off a hot pavement in the sun.

Carmella, he doesn't want you. A sensual woman's voice filled her mind. *He just wants to use you like that pimp, Ramon. They all want to use you and laugh at you and leave you behind.*

"Shut up," she gritted out, concentrating on her finger. The ripples in the air grew more pronounced, and she could see a silvery-gray band on her finger.

You know you're not good for anything more than a roll in the hay. When she didn't respond, it changed tactics. *I can help you make them pay, Carmella. I can make them hurt as much as they hurt you,* the voice continued, velvet and soft in her mind. *I can make Dianta and Branco regret what they've done to you.*

"What are you talking about?" she whispered between her clenched teeth. The ring was almost a solid black now, just strings of silver running through it. It was heavy, and she had to use her other hand to hold her arm.

Who do you think invited me in and used the blood you donated to the Red Cross for the spell? Whose jealousy and desire for power gave you to me? Keep me with you, Carmella.

I can help you bring them to justice like they never imagined.

As she stood trembling, Kell shouted, "Now!"

She stroked her finger over the ring and thought about what the succubus had said. The temptation to accept what it offered tugged at her conscience. Images filled her mind of Dianta crying at her feet and apologizing. All around her, the employees of the samba school cheered as Miguel and Dianta were arrested. She could feel their arms as they hugged her and called her a hero.

Kell yelled at her, "Carmella, please, *now!*"

She stared at him, and it took her a second to figure out why she was here. The succubus hissed inside her mind as Kell's interruption broke the spell of seduction it was weaving around her.

Shuddering at how close she had come to giving into the lies, she ripped the ring off. It tried to squirm out of her fingers before she dropped it into the circle of salt. Her middle finger was red and swollen, as if she had been stung by a bee.

Sean stopped playing the pipe and gripped his sword, moving swiftly to the circle of salt. From the ring, a shape formed, and sand-colored mist shifted and flowed within the boundaries of the circle of salt that now glittered like diamonds. It finally took on the curves of a woman, and its raspy voice filled the air.

"If you let me go, Chosen, I will tell you all I know of their plans. Without me, you will never be able to stop them and Guaricana will kill you all," the succubus whispered into the room.

Carmella held her hand against her chest as she alternated her wide eyes between Sean and the devil. What did it mean by calling Sean "Chosen," and who in the world was Guaricana?

"I don't deal with demons, especially ones that threatened my *Comhcheol*," Sean said with a snarl, the tendons in his arm standing out as his grip on his sword tightened.

"I never harmed her. She's as pure as when I came into her... oh well, she might be responsible, in part, for a few dozen murders... but her body is still pure," the devil mused, twirling gently in its confines of salt. Sean raised the sword over his head, the blessed steel shining in the lamplight. Just before he brought it down, the devil hissed out, "You cannot destroy me, Chosen. I will simply return to the Chaos and await my rebirth."

Using both hands, Sean slammed the sword down onto the carpet, splitting the ring neatly in two. Carmella clasped her hands to her ears as an unearthly shriek made her bones ache. Sean rocked the tip of his sword out of the floor. The white ring of salt was now a scorched black circle.

"Is it gone?" she asked in a faint voice.

"It's gone." Sean moved quickly to her side.

"Okay, I think I'm going to pass—" She didn't even get the chance to finish the sentence before her eyes rolled back.

****

The warmth of sunlight on her eyelids woke Carmella from a deep sleep. The first thing she became aware of was that she was lying on someone's chest. A quick peek confirmed she cuddled against Sean as he slept. She had to suppress a giggle when she heard him snore ever so slightly.

The windows facing the coastline and ocean stood wide open, and she had to appreciate the view. Rio looked much better from twenty stories up. The ocean reflected the oranges and reds of the sunrise, and a few people strolled the white sand beach. She stroked her hand lightly over the red-gold hair on his arm, marveling at the reality of being here with him.

The day should be starting with a chilly shower before boarding the bus for the hour ride to work. Instead, she absorbed the warmth of the most amazing man she had ever met and watched the sunrise. In his sleep, he tucked his arm around her waist and cuddled her closer with a low murmur and a soft smile.

As the sun rose higher in the sky, the need to use the bathroom became urgent enough to take the romance out of listening to his heartbeat as he slept.

Moving slowly, she lifted his arm from her shoulders and padded across the room to the open bathroom door. After taking care of business, she looked at herself in the mirror. For a moment, she just stared at her reflection and ran a wondering fingertip over her face. She looked so different. It wasn't just the lighting or the subdued colors of the walls. She looked at herself clearly for the first time in what seemed like forever.

Leaning forward to peer into the glass, she examined her eyes. Yesterday she had been ashamed at the light brown color. Her mind told her they looked like stupid cow eyes that no man would ever be attracted to. Now she could see the delicate shades of browns and amber and appreciated their depth and complexity. *I'm not ugly. I might not be a beauty queen, but I'm not ugly. Maybe someone who looks like me can interest Sean. Maybe I do have a chance with him.* Smacking her lips together, she made a sour face. She wasn't going to have a chance with anyone if she didn't brush the funk of last night's tequila out of her mouth.

After opening the medicine cabinet, she did her best to brush her teeth with her finger and some toothpaste. Having found some mouthwash, she gave a silent prayer of thanks to whatever god watched over women without toothbrushes.

Sean's voice came through the door as she opened it. He was just hanging up the phone when she shyly stepped out. Even after everything that had happened last night, she hardly knew him. They were at once intimately familiar with each other and strangers.

His eyes lit up and he gave her a charming smile. His hair glowed like fire in the morning sunlight slanting through the windows at his back. "I took the liberty of ordering some room service for us. I thought you might be hungry."

They both stood there awkwardly for a moment, the air taking on a weight against her skin as if light had acquired substance. Gripping her hands into fists, she decided to take charge of the situation. She marched over and placed her hands on Sean's warm chest. He grinned down at her, and she rose on her tippytoes to place a gentle kiss on his stubbly cheek. "Thank you for saving my life."

Cupping her face in one large hand, he said, "You're welcome." She could feel his heart beating fast beneath her palms, and his excitement gave her pleasure.

The beat of her own heart sped as she kissed his other cheek, a slower brush of her lips over his skin. He smelled so good. Whatever aftershave he used was warm on his skin. "Thank you for letting me borrow your clothes."

"You're welcome." His low tone did wonderful things to her body.

Looking into his eyes, she hesitated a moment, drawn in by the emotions she read there. Ever so slowly, she stood on her tiptoes and gently placed her lips against his. A gentle brush of breath and heat, the thinnest of barriers between their skin. It was perfect.

Their lips moved softly over each other, and she wrapped her arms around his neck. He was so strong, and yet he moved against her lips as though she were made of glass.

He stood still against her, but she could feel his heart speed up. His stillness allowed her to be the bold one. She gently stroked her lips against his, moving her hands from around his neck so she could curl them over the tight muscles of his shoulders. With a sigh against his mouth, she traced the muscles of his back and wound her fingers into his hair. Fisting her hands in his hair, she tugged him closer and nipped his lower lip. A savage gleam shone in his gaze and his control snapped. With a low growl he pressed her against him, all that strength holding her gently, in marked contrast to how tight she was holding him.

He felt so good, his kiss firm without bruising, soft without being sloppy. His tongue slipped between her lips, and he fed off the silken moan that escaped her lips. Taking a deep breath, he pulled back and looked down at her, his eyes storm grey with desire. His hard erection pressed against her stomach, and the sensation made her wet.

She gave him a sassy grin. "Thank you for ordering room service. I'm famished." His body tensed against hers, and she couldn't resist doing a slow slide against him. He growled, and she tried to dart away with a challenging grin.

His eyes darkened to slate, and her breath caught in her throat.

"Carmella," her nipples hardened at the way he said her name, "I still have to thank you."

"Oh?" She tried to make it sound light and teasing, but instead her voice took on a husky purr. "What do you have to thank me for?"

Gods, he was overwhelming. He stalked toward her, and she backed away until her knees hit the edge of the bed. Her breath came out in a little sigh as he stopped inches away and slowly pulled off his shirt. The first glimpse of his hard abdominal muscles had her heart pounding, and by the time he tossed the shirt on the floor, she thought she was going to pass out.

He stood still and let her be the one to reach out and touch him. Soft hair, a darker red than that on his head, trailed down from his chest and disappeared into the waistband of his shorts. It felt velvety beneath her fingertips as she ran her palms over the hair of his lower abdomen. The way his muscles tensed and flexed beneath her fingertips made her hormones hum with approval.

Glancing up at him through her lowered lashes, she found him watching her with eyes half closed in pleasure. Her own need made her bold as she slid her hands over his ribs and around to his back, pulling him closer. The back of the bed hit her thighs and she sat on the edge. Spreading her legs, she tugged him between them and gently licked the sensitive skin just beneath his navel.

He twitched in her grasp, and the knowledge that she affected him so deeply burned away any traces of shyness until she was just a creature of warmth and desire. The smooth expanse of his skin felt wonderful against her face as she rubbed her cheek back and forth on his stomach. A little lower, his cock stood out in sharp relief from his shorts. He was a very big man all over.

Kneeling down in front of her, he arched a brow as she pulled her shirt over her head. His eyes widened as her breasts came into view, and he made a growling sound deep in his throat that sent little darts of pleasure through her. As much as she craved his touch, on a deeper level she craved his approval even more. It had been so long since she had let herself connect with anyone, and she was starving for his attention.

Giving her all the time in the world to pull away, he leaned forward until his hot breath against her nipple had her ready to scream in frustration. She wanted him, needed him, now. Memories of their time dancing together surfaced, freed from their spell-imposed prison, and her body ached for his touch. Ached for him to give her the orgasm that Dianta had stolen from her like so much else.

She arched into his mouth, pressing her nipple against his lips. He quickly opened to accept her and lashed at her aching tip, drawing it in and sucking hard. Her whole body shuddered at the sensation, and she held on to his shoulders in a death grip. Teeth, tongue, and heat assaulted her senses until she was rocking against him. Never before had she felt so closely connected to someone and she reveled in not only the physical pleasure he was giving her, but in the intense connection between them. She felt... no longer alone. Complete.

"Thank you for your bravery," he murmured against her skin as he licked his way to her other breast.

Words were beyond her as he continued his assault on her body, raking his teeth over her breast until she thought she would go mad. The center of her world narrowed down to his hard sucks, and when he pulled back, she made a sound of disappointment.

The corners of his lips turned up, and he stood and pushed her back on the bed until she was lying down with her legs hanging over the edge, spread wide by his body. His hands ran down her ribs, touching every inch of her. He didn't have to say what he was thinking; it was in the way he touched her, as if she was the best thing he'd ever felt. His gaze darkened and lust rolled off of him, drowning her in desire. The path of his fingertips had her aching for him and moisture flooded her cleft. He made her feel as though she were flying.

Warm and wet, his lips and tongue worked their way down to her belly button. He licked the little hollow, and she wiggled beneath his mouth.

"Wait, stand up please."

With a curious look he quickly complied and she sat. Not giving herself time to think, she hooked her thumbs into his loose shorts and began to ease them down. She wanted him with a desperation that had her hands shaking at the brief reveal of the skin of his hips and the delicious curve of muscle leading down towards his groin.

Pulling back, he put his hands over hers and stopped her. "You don't have to do that, Carmella."

She snorted and pushed his hands away. "I may be a virgin, but I'm not inexperienced. I'm twenty-three years old, and I've had boyfriends before."

He licked his lower lip in a slow motion that had heat suffusing her body. All of her blood seemed to rush to her pussy, and she felt swollen with need. "Today is about you. What would you like me to do? I want to bring you pleasure like you've never had Carmella. It will satisfy me in ways you'll never know. Help me satisfy you. Tell me what you want." His gaze challenged her, and she knew that he wouldn't go any further unless she was brave enough to say what she wanted.

Silly man, he only knew the Carmella encased in ice. He had no idea how hot her passions ran, especially when she hadn't had an orgasm in what seemed like forever and she was with a man who made her body sing. "Sean, I want you to taste me. I want you to use that talented tongue to make me come."

His nostrils flared, and her shorts were gone so quickly it seemed like magic. She laughed at his exuberance until he hooked her legs over his shoulders and spread her open for his gaze.

All the laughter left her body in a gasp as phantom fingers ruffled through the dark hair covering her mound.

"How..." The words died in her throat as the sensation of teeth scraping against her nipple had her moaning.

He ignored her and ran the tip of his finger down the soft skin of her inner thigh. "Poor baby, you're so wet and swollen. So pretty." The next words were said with his face hovering over her pussy. "Let me take care of you."

The first lick of his tongue had her toes curling and her hips lifting off the bed. He parted her labia with his fingers and gave a second lick, from the crack of her bottom all the way to her aching clit. Slow and rhythmic, he continued to lick her like an ice cream cone, hovering over her clit every third or fourth lick.

Gripping the bedspread beneath her, she couldn't stop the moans that tore from her throat. He was as amazing at this as he was at everything else, and she lost herself in his knowing touch. Spreading her wide with his thumbs and fully exposing her clit, he said something in a language she didn't understand before giving her the softest of touches right onto the sensitive bundle of nerves.

Lightning burned through her veins, and the ache in her body was quickly approaching the point of pain. He nibbled on either side of her clit, gently brushing against it with his nose. As he continued to experiment with her, she tried to rock her hips toward his mouth, to get him to do what she wanted, what she needed.

Tracing circles around her hood with his tongue, he finally licked her directly where she wanted it the most. Her whole body hunched up, muscles so tight they felt as though they would snap. Just before she started swearing at him to make her come, he latched onto her clit and sucked hard.

Each deep pull of his mouth had her writhing on the bed. She dug her heels into the hard muscles of his back, and she could feel him trembling against her. So close, she was almost on the edge. Reality deepened and gained new depth. It was as if time slowed, allowing her to savor every moment, to lose herself in his touch. Drawing in a ragged breath she swore she could taste their passion in the air, as if it were an edible perfume. Sean was beyond amazing and she knew without a doubt that he cherished her. His soul spoke to hers and his adoration swept away the last of her loneliness. Everything ceased to matter except the man between her legs who controlled her world.

When he began to hum as he sucked on her clit, she lost it. The vibration from his lips rivaled that of her best sex toy, and she screamed as she climaxed. White light filled her vision behind her closed eyelids, and pleasure so intense it bordered on pain tore through her body in overwhelming waves. The harsh tone of her scream of pleasure echoed through her mind as her body shamelessly took everything Sean had to offer. She never wanted it to end. She would die if it didn't.

The fierce contractions began to slow down and decrease until the only sound in the room was her panting. He gave her a final lick that had her pushing away from him. She was so sensitive now that anything touching her between her legs was too much.

In a ragged voice he said, "Thank you for trusting me."

A giggle started in her stomach and quickly spilled out of her mouth. She felt so glorious, so alive that she couldn't express it in words. More than that, she felt complete and deliriously happy. And it was all because of Sean.

He crawled up onto the bed next to her and pulled her on top of him. His cock throbbed against her stomach, and the laughter died in her throat. It would feel so good to just jerk his shorts down and straddle him, to give him the part of herself that she had been saving. While some people viewed being a virgin as an inconvenience, she was glad she'd waited for this moment. Sean made her heart sing.

"What about you?" She rolled her hips against him, and he pressed his lips so hard together they turned white.

"Don't worry about me. I'll survive." He took her lips in another consuming kiss until her body was just as aroused as it had been before her orgasm. "Besides, I want to be able to spend days in bed with you."

"Days?" she asked in a faint voice as his hands stroked her bare bottom.

"Months, make that years," he agreed and gripped her ass hard, pulling her close. "No, I mean centuries."

"Oh my," she whispered before nibbling on his neck. While she didn't have his nifty trick of magical phantom hands, she did know how to please a man. Being a virgin didn't mean that she hadn't explored her sexuality—especially how to give her lover just as much pleasure as he gave her. With Sean that might be impossible, but she was going to try her hardest.

He must have read the intent in her face because he groaned and rolled them over onto their sides. "I hate to be the voice of reality," he stroked his lips against her cheek, "but we need to get you out of the city for a few days until we can strengthen your bond with your god."

"What are you talking about?"

With a soft touch he stroked her hair off her cheek. "There is a god or goddess that favors you."

Frowning, she tried to sit up but he pulled her back down. "I don't know what you're talking about. I'm not all that religious."

"Someone, besides me, thinks you're amazing." His gaze softened and her breath caught in her chest at the intense emotions rushing through her. "We both see you as something precious, as our greatest treasure. I will never let anything harm you again, Carmella. I will destroy anyone and anything that tries."

The seriousness in his voice had her licking her lips. Masculine men had always attracted her and she liked it that her man could take care of her. After being forced to only be able to rely on herself, she recognized his offer as something precious. In fact, as odd as it sounded to apply this thought to a man, she found him amazing as well. To have Sean Kalmus, world famous DJ and her hero looking at her with a possessive adoration fanned her desire back into a roaring bonfire. She became desperate for his touch, his kiss.

"Carmella, we don't—"

Before he could finish his sentence, she had him flipped over onto his back and had straddled his hips. The slide of his cock through the slick satin of his shorts had her arching her back and purring out a moan.

He gripped her hips and trembled. "Carmella."

The rest of whatever he was going to say came out in a low moan as she rocked against him. As wet as she was, she bet he could feel her arousal soaking onto his shaft. She reveled in the sense of power and control pleasing him gave her. It had been far too long since she had felt this much like herself.

Leaning down to kiss him, she stiffened as his hands rocked her hips over his erection. If he didn't stop soon she was going to lose herself in another orgasm, and as wonderful as that idea was, she wanted to make him lose control. His skin held a faint hint of salt as she licked her way down his neck, reminding her again of the ocean. The sensation of his hands running up and down her back had her sighing against his skin.

Gazing at his impressive body, she licked her lips and admired him. Long and lean muscles graced his body, the frame of an athlete rather than that of a body builder. She ran her hands over him greedily, trying to touch as much of his body as she could. Her out of control response wasn't just the sensuality of being with him but also the universal comfort of touching another human being. She hadn't realized until now how much she had missed the simple feel of a warm body against hers.

Anger tried to gain a foothold in her mind, but she pushed it away. Later there would be time for revenge; now it was about love. That thought startled her even as she kissed her way down his stomach, pausing to lick at his belly button. Did she love him? That was impossible, wasn't it? She had known him for only a few days, but there was no denying the feeling of completion that being with him brought to her heart. He filled an aching void so completely that it seemed as though he'd always been there.

The crisp auburn hairs beneath his belly button tickled against her nose as she ran her tongue along the edge of where his shorts met his stomach. He murmured something in words she didn't understand but in a tone that made her smile. So much desire in his voice, so much need. She tugged his shorts down, and he eagerly lifted his hips for her.

The sight of his cock made her pussy clench. Long and thick, the head was a deep rose color, and veins stood out along his length. He placed his arms behind his head and leaned up to watch her. Knowing that he was enjoying the sight, she gently grasped him by the base and gave the head one slow lick. The strangled noise he made sent bolts of glittering lust through her before she lay down between his muscular thighs and rubbed herself against the sheets.

She had missed this so much. The pleasure between a man and a woman was one of the ultimate gifts of the gods, and she intended to honor their present. His thighs tensed on either side of her as she took him into her mouth and slowly sank down on him until he hit the back of her throat. Energy vibrated from his body, and she made a startled noise around his length as his magic pressed between her legs like strong fingers.

The sensation of a fingertip twirling around her clit had her sucking him hard in rhythm with the phantom touch. This kind of intense blending of sensations was beyond anything she had imagined, and she felt herself being carried away. Cupping his sac gently, she cradled the full weight and delighted in how his balls drew taut beneath her touch. A firm pinch on her clit had her bucking while he wrapped his legs around her back to hold her still, and his low, deep laughter stroked against her soul.

In the darkness behind her eyelids, she existed in a world of touch and sensation. His energy wrapped around her like a living blanket, drawing her closer to her own orgasm, even as she strived to bring his. She could feel him, feel the edge of his lust as he drew near his peak. Male and rough, it had a wilder edge than her own pleasure, and she trembled against his body. She wrapped her hand around his shaft and stroked him as she sucked, twirling her tongue over the head.

Invisible lips locked around her clit and pulled, bringing her orgasm so quickly she was writhing against his body as she struggled to breathe around his hard length in her mouth. The warm spasms of her release continued, being drawn out with such skill that she saw sparkles of green and gold behind her eyelids. His hips lifted beneath her, and she took him as deep as she could as the beginning of his orgasm rushed through her.

Gods, she could feel an echo of his pleasure and delighted in drawing every spurt out of him until he shook beneath her. She released him with one final lick and didn't protest when he pulled her up next to him. Naked, they curled around each other and she let herself float. So amazing. Even now his energy brushed against her body like the softest fur imaginable. The warm sunlight streaming through the window felt heavenly on her back as he gently kissed her forehead.

No words were needed. He touched her with such reverence that she felt as though she was going to burst with joy. Stroking her hand along his cheek, she looked into his eyes and forgot to breathe, seeing the depth of his warm and intense emotions in their swirling blue depths. Bright and pure, he looked at her as if she was the most beautiful thing in the world. Light to her darkness, an ocean of warmth to chase away the desert of cold that had been her heart.

His cell phone played an intricate melody, and he groaned, burying his face in her hair. Reaching over the edge of the bed, he grabbed their discarded clothes and then pulled the shirt over her head. "Get dressed before I say to hell with the world and just lock the door."

Quickly tugging at the shirt, she bent to pull the shorts over her still buzzing pussy. He cleared his throat, and she couldn't help but grin at the tortured expression on his face as he watched her breasts bounce while she put the shorts on. Oh yes, she would love to spend the rest of her life getting to know his body, to know what turned him on and what made him lose control. It seemed as though all she had to do was look at him and liquid warmth pooled between her legs.

He pulled her off the bed and into the circle of his arms. Never had she felt more safe or cherished. "Where is your god's temple?"

She chewed her lip and stroked the firm muscles of his forearms. "Umm, Sean. I don't think I have a god."

He looked down at her in surprise. "Of course you do. His blessing glitters all over your aura."

"Huh?" was the most intelligent thing she could come up with. She wanted to rub her cheek against his and taste his skin.

He leaned down and whispered against her lips, "Your aura. It's beautiful and the color of the first violets of spring."

"Oh, that's nice." She sighed as he gently stroked his hands up the side of her neck. It made her eyes shut, and she leaned back into his touch. His large hand traced the edge of her jaw and over her lips.

"You're so beautiful. Your skin is softer than anything I have ever touched." He slowly ran his thumb over her sensitive lower lip. She nipped at his thumb and wet it with the tip of her tongue. His groan traveled through her ears and settled between her thighs in a deep throb.

Her reply was cut off by a knock at the door and a shout. "Sean, we need to hit the road. Monica just called from the samba school. Dianta is questioning everyone about where Carmella is and freaking out."

He gave her cheek one more soft stroke. "Let's go find your god."

Chapter Eight

Three things happened at once. Sean let Kell into the suite, room service arrived, and Sean's cell phone began to ring. Kell took care of the room service while Sean answered his phone, tipping the hotel worker, and then lifted the lids to sniff at the eggs and waffles.

Giving Kell a shy smile, she snagged a waffle off the plate and nibbled on it while she watched Sean. He was gazing out the window and talking quietly into the phone, his posture tense.

She gave Kell a questioning look, but he only shrugged and continued to eat. She shuffled her feet in the pair of complimentary shower flip-flops. Anything was better than those six-inch heels, so she didn't complain about the neon green foam flip-flops.

Sean hung up the phone and looked out the window for a minute.

Kell called over from the breakfast tray, "Hey, if you're hungry, you better get over here before your harmony eats all the food." Kell pretended not to see her flip him the bird, and she slathered syrup over a heavily buttered waffle.

"Carmella." Sean still faced the window with his hands clasped behind his back. "Do you know someone named Tian?"

The waffle turned into dry foam in her mouth. Making an effort to swallow past her fear, she said, "Yeah. He's a friend of mine who works at the samba school."

"I thought so." Sean turned around. His face was grim and his shoulders tight. "That was Dianta on the phone. She has Tian and Monica. She wants to exchange them for you."

She swallowed hard, rage and fear mixing as she thought of all the terrible things Dianta could be doing to Monica and Tian right now.

Kell locked eyes with Sean. "Uh-uh, no way we are sending Carmella to them. They can kiss my hairy white arse. We'll find some way to rescue them. I—"

Sean cut him off and tried to hide his worry as he glanced at her "I think we can still gain the upper hand, Kell. We just need her to be our Trojan horse."

"Whatever you need me to do, I'm game." She felt a tear of anger run down her cheek and had to stifle back a sob at the thought of Tian being tortured. "This is partially my fault." Her voice broke, and she continued, "The succubus told me last night that Dianta and Branco are responsible for my possession. I fainted and then...forgot about it this morning," She hung her head with guilt.

"Who is Branco?"

"A bad, bad man." She took a deep breath and let it out slowly, trying to still her racing heart. "Rumor has it that he's big time into black magic and very powerful. The succubus said he's the one that cursed me, along with Dianta."

With a grunt Kell pushed back from the table and stood. "Makes sense. Dianta certainly doesn't have the power to summon a succubus. Sean, do you think he's a Chosen?"

"I don't know, but he could be." Sean swore softly. "If he's a Chosen of Guaricana then things just got really dangerous."

She gave a harsh laugh. "You mean they aren't dangerous now?"

"We have to assume that Branco has some kind of powerbase in the city or nearby. If he does, then not only are we facing another Chosen, but we're facing a Chosen on his home turf." He exchanged a look with Kell. "Maybe you should take Carmella somewhere safe."

"No!" Both men looked at her with a startled expression and she lowered her voice. "No, I'm coming with you. This all happened because of me. If something happens to Tian it will be all my fault."

Sean unclenched his fists and took her face in his hands, forcing her to look at him. "This is not your fault. This was done by sick, evil people who would be doing this to someone else if you weren't here. We don't have time to fight about this, so if you're coming with me I need you to be as strong as possible, to tap into your patron god's energy and protection. Can you think of any god or goddess that you've interacted with? Anything that could point us in the right direction?"

Her mind jumped from image to horrible image of all the painful things that could have been done to Tian and Monica while they stood here eating breakfast. "I don't know. I don't worship any gods. That's my mother. She—" The memory of the last time she had seen her mother sounded through her mind like a clear chime. "I know who it is," she whispered. "I haven't thought about him in a long time, but my mother gave me a statue of the Egyptian god, Bes. It's been in our family for generations on her side, and we used to dance for his glory when I was growing up. I never thought it was real. I just loved to dance with my mother."

Sean blew out a breath through his nose. "Okay. Kell, search on the Internet for information about Bes. I don't know much about the Egyptian pantheon, and we need to figure out how to contact him and where we can find a temple around here."

"Got it, boss. I'll call our people in town and let them know to stick together." Kell started to leave the room, but Carmella stopped him with a surprisingly strong grip.

"I know where we can find a statue of Bes. Would that work?"

Sean smiled, and her heart did a flutter. "Yeah, that would work just fine. Where is it?"

The old feelings of shame at her tiny apartment came back. With a mental shove, she pushed the feeling of inadequacy away. They didn't have time for her pride, or lack thereof. Tian could be dying. Who cared if her dishes didn't match and her bathroom had only an old shower? "It's at my apartment. My mother gave it to me before I left home."

Sean grabbed his wallet and keys off the counter. "Excellent. Kell, get your laptop and your goodie bag. Carmella and I will meet you downstairs in the Land Rover."

****

Sean pulled the expensive SUV to a stop in front of Carmella's apartment complex. As usual the street was crowded with people. Some merely going about their business and others constantly on the lookout for either the police or the opportunity to make some easy money. She'd grown used to the constant hustle of the prostitutes and drug dealers, but her heart sank a bit as she wondered what Sean thought of her neighborhood. While some of the apartments were behind thick walls, like her own, others had open courtyards that faced the street. In those yards gang leaders would hold court and when Sean parked the high end SUV she could see the gang members and hustlers watching with interest. When Sean and Kell got out of the SUV, Sean took a charm out of his pocket and looped it around the antenna.

"This is an antitheft impotence charm," Sean said loud enough for everyone to hear. "If anyone touches this car before I remove it, they can forget ever having to worry about using a condom again. And for the women, any man you touch will never be able to rise to the occasion."

Carmella repeated his words in Portuguese, laughing to herself at the stricken looks on the young men's faces. Word would spread fast, and Sean's SUV wouldn't be on blocks as soon as they turned their backs.

She led them up the stairs to her apartment. Taking a deep breath, she opened the door and started to apologize right away. "I'm sorry it's so small. I know you're used to better places, and I don't have air-conditioning. I'm sorry it isn't—"

Sean cut her off with a kiss, soft and sure, his long artistic fingers smoothing down her throat to trace her collarbone through her shirt. It made her tremble, and soft waves of pleasure followed his lips and hands like the light trail from a sparkler.

Delicate kisses over the line of her jaw led his lips to her ear. The rasp of his stubble against her skin was exquisite. "Didn't anyone ever tell you it's not the size that counts?" Sean whispered into her ear, his warm breath making her shiver and reach for him as she laughed.

Stepping back, Sean took a deep breath and tapped Kell on the shoulder. "Okay, Kell. You can turn around now."

Kell fixed both of them with a glare. "If you two could keep your hands off each other in front of me, it would be appreciated."

Sean snorted as she blushed. "If I had a pound for every time I had to watch you and Mary go at it like two horny teenagers—"

"That's different," Kell said grumpily with a sniff.

"Why is that?"

"Because it's me and not you." Kell gave Sean a merry smile.

She shook her head and walked with a much lighter heart to the little shelf where she kept the statue. Moving carefully, she cradled the stone in her arms. The meaning of the statue Bes took on a completely new significance. She stood before them and held out the statue. "Well, this is it—I mean him."

Both men stared at the carving with a strange mixture of awe and disbelief. "Doesn't look very Egyptian," Sean said finally.

Kell grinned and shook his head. "Nope, that's how the websites described him. He can either be in the form of a lion or a short, muscular dwarf with a long beard."

"Be nice to Bes." She cradled the statue to her chest defensively.

"Interesting, the sparkles around your aura flared when you defended your god. He's listening to you." Sean turned to Kell. "So, how does Bes accept tribute?"

"Well, he's mainly a war god, but he's also a patron of the pleasures of the home. Whatever that means." Kell shrugged. "I didn't have much time to read, and oddly enough, they don't have WiFi out here."

"A war god?" Sean asked as he gave her a wicked grin that made her toes curl. "I couldn't have asked for a better advantage than that."

"I know how to worship him." She smiled back at Sean. Being happy around him was as natural as breathing. "My mother said since I'm not married I can't do offerings of drinking—and stuff you do with your husband." Her eyes darted to Sean, who looked very interested. "But I can dance to his glory."

"Okay, great. Do you have a CD player or something we can use?" Kell asked.

"No, I, uh, well, I can't really afford many luxuries at the moment." She turned her head to look out the window, hoping they wouldn't notice the shame heating her face.

"Carmella, do you have any musical instruments?" Sean asked gently. "I have my flute, but for this kind of ceremony we will need a drum."

Her shoulders sagged. "No, I don't." She tried to desperately think of something they could use. If worse came to worst, she had a bucket they could use as a drum. "Wait, Mrs. Amável has a drum that her husband used to use. I bet she would let us borrow it."

Sean took the statue from her. "Then let's go make nice to Mrs. Amável. We need to strengthen your bond to Bes and go find our people."

Fifteen minutes later, Carmella stared at the statue of Bes, now standing on the edge of a wilted flowerbed. She tried to ignore the crowd of people watching from their windows or sitting on the steps. Word had spread about Carmella and her visitors, and one of the women had recognized Sean as DJ Kal.

Mrs. Amável had lent them the drum. Carmella told her she needed to practice a dance for the Carnival. At that, Mrs. Amável had begged to watch Carmella dance, saying it had been so long since she had been to the ballet. Mr. Amável used to take her all the time, but she didn't feel right going without him. Catching Sean's quick nod, Carmella graciously invited Mrs. Amável and Gabriel outside to watch them in the garden area in the front of the building.

Her heart slammed in her ribs, and sweat began to trail down her back. She had quickly changed into a pair of denim shorts and a purple tank top. A lilac belly-dancing scarf festooned with silver coins lay limp in her hands. Out of the corner of her eye, she watched the women lean out of their windows. Some took pictures with their cell phones while a few others had video cameras rolling.

Suddenly, they began to whistle and do catcalls that echoed between the buildings. Turning around, she watched Sean finish taking his shirt off. Her breath caught in her throat. The most intricate tattoo she had ever seen blazed across his back. It was beautiful. She followed the twisting knot pattern with her eyes and had a brief fantasy about following it with her tongue. He sat down on the dusty ground nearby and placed the large drum between his legs.

Kell sat in the shade of the front porch, scratching Gabriel behind his ears. The dog had taken an immediate liking to both men, offering his soft tan belly with a happy doggy grin.

Closing her eyes and turning away, she let out a small laugh. She wasn't nervous about dancing in front of all these people anymore. Instead, she was nervous about dancing in front of the man who astounded her and filled her empty heart. Gathering her courage, she tied the scarf around her hips and gave it a shake. The coins sewn into it tinkled as they tapped against each other.

Sean's movements captured her attention as he stretched out his hands and arms. The muscles of his forearms moved and rippled beneath his pale skin, and she appreciated the lightest brush of freckles on his shoulders. Following the line of his throat, she captured his gaze and sighed at the heat there. He quirked a fair eyebrow and gave her a slow grin that made her want to drag him back to her apartment. His low chuckle filled the air as he watched her stare at him, and a few giggles came from the porch.

She gave Sean a bland look before pulling off her tank top. She stood before him in her sports bra, resisting the urge to cover herself as he gave her a long, slow appraisal. Obviously, he liked what he saw. The desire in his look scorched her, and his lips softened as if anticipating a kiss. A bead of sweat rolled down the soft curve of her belly, and he followed its track to the belt around her hips.

There was more laughter and some cheering from the women of the apartment complex. This display of teasing and dominance was well understood. *Why, this is like dancing the carimbó, except I'll be trying to seduce him with my dancing while he'll try to seduce me with his music.* The thought gave her a sudden confidence, a familiar way to address this awkward, yet exciting, situation. She lifted her chin and threw her shoulders back, every inch a woman secure with her own sexuality and power while she looked Sean in the eye.

Sean's lips curved into an appreciative smile, and he began to beat on the drum.

She undulated her belly in a slow, easy roll. The steady beat matched the rhythm of her heart, and she rocked her hips in large flowing circles, isolating her muscles so her chest stayed still. Sean's eyes locked onto her body, and she allowed herself a satisfied smile. He never faltered with the beat, but he shifted and took a deep breath.

Power, that was what she felt as she turned to the statue of Bes—the power of being a woman, embracing the beauty and sensuality that was a woman's unique gift. There was no shame in being an object of love and desire. In this time and place, it was a sacred celebration of joy.

Sean's magic began to flow through the drumbeats. It lifted the hair on her arms and filled her body with a delicious energy she never knew existed. Around them, some women began to cry while others threw their heads back and laughed. The dance and the music deeply affected each of them in its own way. Every woman remembered she was worth something and that she was a miracle. As a child of Creation, no one should ever forget how special they are.

Her eyelids fluttered shut as Bes's grace moved over her in a soft wave. In her mind, she saw a lion sitting in the middle of the desert, his massive paws crossed as he watched over his enormous pride. They were his children, and he loved them well. In her vision, she danced before the pride of lions, aware of their massive strength and potential for violence. The sand crunched beneath her feet, and she felt the desert air drying the sweat on her skin.

Was she a lioness of the pride? No, that didn't feel right. The music moved her, and she twirled to its pounding beat. She was a cub, cherished and protected, loved and sheltered as she stumbled her way through life.

"That is what I am," she whispered into the hot desert silence of her vision. "I'm your child."

As this thought spilled out of her mouth, the lion stood up. He was huge, bigger than any cat she had ever seen in the zoo. His brown mane ruffled in the breeze, and his golden-bronze eyes saw into her soul. She dropped to her knees and put her forehead to the sand. His gaze was too strong to hold. Her brain couldn't begin to describe what his eyes contained. His gaze held all the love in the universe, all the pride and glory of war, all the comforts and sensuality of the home.

As she huddled in the hot sand, his roar washed over her. It hid words for her ears alone. *I have missed you, my daughter. Welcome home. I give you my gifts for the fight ahead. Use them well. You're my tool for answering the prayers of many wounded hearts.*

For a long moment she floated in a soft golden mist, wrapped in arms so vast she knew nothing would ever harm her here. Slowly, the mist faded, and she realized the golden light was the sun shining through her eyelids. Sean's strong arms held her close as his voice rumbled against her ear. "Give her a minute, she's all right. She's communing with her god."

Opening her eyes, she turned her head and smiled. The women around her gasped quietly, and one began to cry in choked sobs. She could still feel his blessing within her, and she knew what she had to do here before they left. Gently, she pulled herself out of Sean's arms. He gave her a brilliant smile and said softly, "You glow with his grace."

She felt a deep peace settle over her. She turned to the crowd and sought out the hearts calling to her. They needed his blessing, but they were lost and couldn't find it without her. Touching arms and shoulders as she passed, she came to stand before a middle-aged woman with tears streaming down her cheeks.

She gently took the woman's face in her hands and placed a kiss on her forehead. A bright spark of magic moved from her lips to the woman, and she knew the right words to say. With a soft whisper into her ear, she said, "The death of your baby wasn't your fault, Saria. Forgive yourself, and there will be children in your future."

The woman gasped and squeezed her hand, but she was already moving away.

"What is going on?" Mrs. Amável asked in a hushed whisper.

"She's god-touched," Kell rumbled. "She's filled with Bes's blessing and is doing his work on Earth."

Carmella stopped in front of another woman who wrung her fingers so hard she was leaving scratches on the backs of her hands. Very young and wearing a hot-pink dress that showed more than it concealed, her heavy makeup streaked down her face as she cried. She watched Carmella approach with wide, desperate eyes.

The tone of her voice was one of infinite peace and kindness. "Your father misses you, Veviri. Go home to him. Your childhood sweetheart, Jose, is waiting for you." The woman began to protest, and Carmella laid a gentle hand over her lips. "Do not let excuses and shame shackle you here to men who abuse you. Go home and let yourself be loved."

Gliding across the hot concrete, she came to a stop before Sean and Kell. The sense of peace vanished from her soul, righteous fury taking its place. "Let's go get our people," she said quietly, and all who heard her voice trembled.

Chapter Nine

Sean fended off Gabriel's sloppy kisses. "Carmella, Dianta said you would know where they are."

Carmella frowned and looked toward the street. "I know what it looks like. It's a club with two giant dice done in white neon out front. I think it's a private club. The door had no handle on the outside." Bitter, frightening memories assailed her mind, leaving her sickened inside as she realized how long the succubus had been using her. "I've had nightmares about this place for months. I never imagined it actually existed, but that's where Bes says they are."

Sean swore softly. "It could take us days to find it. We don't have that kind of time." He turned to Kell. "Who can we contact locally who—"

"Excuse me," a sweet voice mumbled hesitantly.

Carmella glanced over at one of the prostitutes who lived in the building. She wore a pair of dirty cut-off sweats and an old T-shirt. Thin to the point of looking ill, she scratched at the track marks on her arms. "I wasn't eavesdropping, but I know the club you're talking about."

They all turned to look at her, and the woman clasped her hands nervously in front of them. Speaking to the ground, she said, "It's an S&M club. One of my...dates likes to go there. I don't do anything, but he pays me to watch him get whipped. It's on Riachuelo Street across from the Academia Santana. Go down the alley on the left between the cobblers and the bookstore. The entrance is hidden behind some dumpsters. It's hard to see from the street."

"I know where that is." Carmella pulled her tank top back on. "We can be there in fifteen minutes." She took the woman's hand in her own, and Bes's blessing warmed within her again. "Thank you, little one. You are stronger and kinder than you know. If you will allow me, I would like to give you a gift."

"It's okay." The woman tried to pull her hand away as shame filled her eyes. "Watching you dance made me feel better than I have in a long, long time."

Carmella smiled and gently cupped her face. "Close your eyes." Softly, she placed a kiss on the woman's lips, once again that bright spark of magic flared between them as Bes's blessing was given to the woman.

Carmella pulled back, and the woman shuddered and clutched her stomach. Sean and Kell were about to go to her when she looked up, tears running down her face. "The craving, it's gone. I've been addicted to heroin for over four years now, but the craving, that demon of addiction, it's gone."

The gate chinked open as Carmella called over her shoulder, "Mrs. Amável, if I don't come back, please give my apartment to someone who needs it."

Mrs. Amável raised her hand in acknowledgment, her arms around the prostitute as she wept.

****

They stood in front of the black-painted door, the twist in Carmella's stomach confirming this was the right club.

"This place is nasty." Kell hitched the gun belt around his thick waist and spat over his shoulder. The smell of hot garbage filled the air, and a thick black liquid seeped from one of the containers.

Kell and Sean stood armed and ready, but she had no experience with guns. Instead, she had a long, curved knife in a brown leather sheath clipped to her shorts. If worse came to worst, she could pull the blade and not have to worry about a safety lock. Sean had his sword sheathed around his back and the small silver flute in his front pocket.

Kell pulled his fingers through his beard. "How many people are inside, Sean?"

"I don't know. Someone has a shield on the club, and it's strong. Every once in a while I get a hint of a bad psychic smell, so I think there is a Destruction Chosen inside."

"Oh, for the love of the gods. This just gets better and better." Kell groaned and nervously ran a thumb over the hammer of the pistol on his belt.

She remained silent, their words a distant sound; her mind was focused on other things. A breath of hot desert air blew over her, clearing away the muggy stink of the garbage bins. She looked at the door and *knew* how to get inside. It wasn't as though Bes had whispered in her ear. Instead, she had the strategic mindset of a seasoned warrior. Looking around the alley she found herself analyzing every inch of the club, knowing where she should go if they were attacked for the best chance at defense and cataloging the items around them that could be used as weapons. Her mind raced through different fight scenarios, providing her with information so fast that she could barely process it. At first it was scary, but slowly she realized she was still herself. It wasn't like when the succubus took her over. She was still Carmella, just—more.

"Sean, you need to play the door down. Like that story in the Bible about the trumpet taking down the walls of the city," she said in a quiet voice, scanning the bricks around the door. Traffic passed occasionally at the end of the alley, but the view was obstructed by a series of large dumpsters.

Kell gaped at her, but Sean gave her a proud smile, and she grinned back at him. "It would be my pleasure to play for you."

She blew him a kiss and stepped back, unsure how exactly the door would come down. If it was going to explode, she wanted to be out of the line of fire.

Licking his lips, Sean focused on the door and began to play a fierce tune on the flute. The frame around the door and then the metal vibrated. Kell and Carmella exchanged a wide-eyed glance and watched as the door began to melt. The door and frame deconstructed itself into a pile of metal shavings and black paint chips.

The sunlight shining through revealed a typical set of tacky red barstools, black tile floors, and a small hostess stand. No monsters of darkness like in her dreams. Kell took out his boot knife and chipped out human teeth from the inside of the doorframe. One had a filling in it and another looked too small to belong to an adult. Kell kicked the teeth into the pile of shaved metal. "The wardings are down. Gods of Creation, help the poor souls who died to make it."

Carmella started to walk into the club, but Sean laid a hand on her shoulder. "Let me go first, my harmony," he said in a gentle voice, his gaze already on the entrance.

She tilted her head and examined his profile. "Okay, but you have to tell me what this harmony thing is about when we get out of here."

Sean gave her a roguish smile that made her toes curl. "We have many things to discuss once we get out of here."

Her heart skipped a beat and then sped a rapid pace as she read the emotion in his eyes. With her heightened senses, she could feel his love for her. It was as warm as the spring sun on her skin.

Giving her shoulder a squeeze, Sean stepped through the door. Kell covered his back in a shooter's stance, and she toyed with the hilt of her knife as she followed the men inside.

Searching the wall next to the door, she flicked a switch, and the lights came on. Something smelled bad in here, not just the usual spilled beer and cheap perfume smell of a bar, but something rotten.

"Gah, what's that?" Kell murmured.

Sean took a slow breath and grimaced. "Smells like death and suffering."

"Great," she muttered as they moved farther into the room, following the curve of the metal and glass bar. Shackles and chains hung from thick black rods crisscrossing the ceiling. There were wood- and leather-covered devices propped against the wall that she couldn't even imagine a use for. A set of stocks like something from a medieval movie set stood on a small raised stage. Instead of wood, they were made out of thick, clear plastic and stood illuminated beneath a soft spotlight.

The closer they came to a stairway leading to the lower level, the heavier the rot in the air became. It reminded her of a package of hamburger that had been left in the fridge too long. On either side of the stairs stood long display cases lit like a jewelry store. Instead of diamonds and pearls, the velvet beds held ball gags, hoods, cuffs, whips, and the largest assortment of sex toys she had ever seen.

"Remind me to grab something for the wife before we leave." Kell gave a nervous laugh and examined an assortment of latex dildos shaped like fists and feet.

They ignored him and stared at the entrance to the stairs. The walls here were painted a shiny black, and metal-framed photographs of black-and-white bondage scenes led the way down. At the base of the stairs were bathrooms and an open doorway leading to the left.

"Let me guess. We get to go down the dark, creepy stairs and into the dark, creepy basement?" She tried to breathe through her mouth and inched closer to Sean.

Sean nodded and held his hand to his lips. "At least three people down there. It's still hard to tell. Something is blocking me."

They slowly made their way down the stairs, every creak and groan of the wood making her tension wind tighter until her shoulders were rigid and her back ramrod straight. The lights were on down here as well, and from behind the closed white door down the hall to the left came the sound of muffled music.

Kell raised his gun and pointed it to the door at the end of the hall. "What's the plan, boss?" he said in a quiet voice.

The hair on her arms stood up. An electrical current moved through the air and brought with it the smell of a deep forest. Taking a deep breath, she tracked the source of the smell to Sean who currently had his eyes closed while his lips moved as they formed exotic words in a language she couldn't place. She went to touch his arm, but Kell grabbed her hand and stopped her.

Kell pulled her close and whispered in her ear, "Sean is talking to his god Maponus. When a god is talking to someone, it's a good idea not to interrupt."

After a moment, Sean opened his eyes and gazed at them. A hint of golden lighting flickered through his eyes, and she gasped. "We are to go into the room and let Carmella do her thing."

Silence met his statement. "My thing?" she squeaked out. "What the hell is my thing?"

Sean shrugged and unsheathed his blade. "I don't know. I asked Maponus, and he said Bes had it under control."

"Fantastic," she whispered as she unsheathed the dagger from her waist. The hilt felt right in her hand, and she twirled the blade in the light, enjoying the weight of it against her palm.

With a nod from Kell, they moved down the hall to stand before the white door. No magical booby traps turned them into frogs. To her, it looked like an ordinary door, one that would be found in any home. The normalcy of it made it seem even more out of place in the S&M club setting.

Sean took a deep breath and nudged the door open with his foot. It took her a moment to process the scene inside of the room. Her mind wanted to reject it as fake, something from a cheesy horror movie with a low budget but a lot of fake blood. A weird song played from speakers somewhere in the room. The foul and grating language rang unfamiliar in her ears, and it made her head throb.

Dianta and Branco lounged on two red velvet chairs placed on a dais and presided over the room. Dianta wore a chain and leather outfit that looked like the costume from some cheap porno while Branco reclined in his usual dark suit. Grisly remains of people in various states of decay hung from the walls. She was able to piece together at least six bodies before she stopped counting. More bodies decomposed in a pile in the far corner of the room, tossed aside like garbage, a tangle of limbs and hair.

Next to Dianta, Tian hung suspended from a large wooden X, his hands and feet secured to the beams by shackles. His head drooped to the side, and his back had been whipped to the muscle in some places. Breath still moved through his lungs, but it was shallow and uneven.

Carmella let out a low moan. Spinning to face Dianta, Carmella called her and her mother every bad thing she could think of in Portuguese at the top of her lungs. Dianta launched herself from the chair, her fake nails curled like claws, but Branco placed a hand on her arm, and she sat back down, fuming.

The room felt wrong, cold, as if Carmella were standing in a freezer. Her breath didn't fog the air, so she assumed it must be something she felt with her soul. "Sean, why is it so cold in here?" Carmella whispered as Branco and Sean studied each other.

Tilting his head in her direction, Sean said, "The souls of the men they killed here are trapped in this room. Branco is using them for power. Until they are released, they are in a state of eternal torment. You're feeling their pain."

Carmella suppressed a shudder and tightened her hand on the knife.

"So, you're the Chosen of Maponus," Branco drawled out. "I expected someone more... scary."

"And you're the Chosen of Guaricana. I expected someone less cheesy," Sean said with a merry smile.

Branco's teeth came together with an audible snap. "How dare you insult me! My god will flay the flesh from your pasty back. He will—"

"Yeah, yeah, big and scary, I get it." Sean crossed his arms. "Tell me, why isn't your god here right now, Branco? Surely he feels your distress. Why isn't he helping you?" Sean asked as he leaned on his sword.

Branco stiffened. "He's always with me." A snide and cruel smile came over his face. "He usually likes men, but your little woman Monica inspired him with her screams."

Sean's shoulders tightened even as he kept his tone casual. "Really? Where is Monica?"

"Oh, I'm afraid we played too rough with her." Dianta smirked at Carmella. She leaned over and ran a finger down Tian's unresponsive body, licking his blood from her fake nail. "Her corpse is somewhere on the floor around here." She made a negligent wave with her hand toward the pile of bodies in the corner. Sorrow filled Carmella at the sight of Monica's slender form covered in blood, tossed aside like a broken doll.

Kell screamed and fired at them, but his bullets hit some kind of invisible shield and melted into red-hot puddles of metal on the floor. The pitch of the music increased, and Carmella huddled to the floor as her nose began to bleed. Sean and Kell struggled to remain upright as blood dripped from their noses.

Dianta laughed and clapped her hands while Branco just smiled. Carmella watched in horrified fascination, unable to move as her blood began to pool beneath her face.

Sean groaned. "Kell, shoot the speakers."

Sweat broke out on the other man's face, his breathing labored as he fought to speak. "Fuck...can't move. So strong."

"Pray," Sean managed to choke out past the blood now pouring down his face.

Kell's arm wavered then firmed, and he shot at two black speakers in the corners of the room. The chanting stopped, and Carmella slid in her own blood as she tried to stand. Her hand trembled as she wiped her blood off her lip and chin with the edge of her shirt.

Carmella felt as though she was having a waking dream. The bodies hanging on the walls no longer seemed real as she glared Dianta. A whisper of power, warm as the desert winds, moved through her mind. She knew how to get through the shield, and her heart demanded retribution for the pain Dianta had caused. Placing a hand on Sean's arm, she leaned and whispered into his ear, "I can get the shield down. Can you handle Branco while I deal with Dianta?"

Sean studied her intently, his slate-blue eyes searching hers. He nodded and placed a gentle kiss on her lips. Beside them Kell spat blood onto the floor and tried to wipe it out of his beard.

"Oh, please," Dianta complained. "Is that why the succubus was kicked out? Did you go after Sean like a bitch in heat?" She gave Carmella a leer and made an obscene tongue gesture that reminded Carmella of a thirsty lizard.

Bes moved Carmella's body, overtaking her control and leaving her as an observer of her body's actions. Unlike the possession of the succubus, Carmella was fully aware of what was going on. She trusted Bes completely and relinquished total control. Not taking her eyes off Dianta, Carmella walked to the edge of the shield. She could feel its energy humming off her skin, cold and full of hurt. She knelt down to the floor and watched her hand wet itself with the blood there.

Sean and Kell stood behind her as she held her hand up and began to trace hieroglyphs onto the invisible barrier, bloody symbols appearing to float in the air.

Dianta surged out of her chair and stood behind Branco's mock throne. "What is she doing!" she screeched.

Branco stood and held his cane in one scarred hand. "Somehow, that bitch is going to break the shield."

Carmella continued to draw symbols as Sean hummed behind her, adding strength to her spell with his own magic. Rage was moving through her body, the pure, clean anger of the righteous. Dianta must pay, not only for giving Carmella to the succubus but also for the deaths of all of these people just to further her own ego-driven plans. As she finished, her eyes locked onto Dianta, and she mouthed, "You're mine."

Dianta squeaked and teetered back on her ridiculous platform heels. Smearing her hands with Tian's blood, Dianta brought them together and began to chant. Branco didn't even look at Carmella, instead walking off the dais and keeping his gaze locked on Sean. Obviously, he didn't think she was a threat. Stupid man.

The control of her body returned in a rush, but she still sensed Bes's divine power moving through her. Words whispered into her mind, images of what she must do if she wanted to save Tian. Gathering her resolve, she said in a trembling voice, "Once the shield goes down, Kell, you need to free Tian and get him out of here. Sean, keep Branco off me long enough to do what I need to do."

"But you aren't..." Kell protested, his voice dying off as he looked into Carmella's gaze and his eyes grew wide with wonder. Whatever he saw there seemed to reassure him and he actually smiled. His shoulders snapped back, and he said in a calm voice, "Okay."

The shield let out a hum that made her teeth vibrate, and Carmella's head whipped back as her body absorbed the shock of the shield falling. The hieroglyphs melted off the air and back into the puddle of blood on the floor.

Branco jerked a long rapier out of his cane and held it in front of his body. "You'll never walk out of here, Sean. I'll use your skull as a toilet," he snarled as he sliced through the air fast enough to make the blade sing.

"You know what one of the worst parts of being Chosen is?" Sean quipped with a smirk as he held his sword before him. "I have to listen to all these melodramatic speeches about how my death is coming blah blah blah. Yet here I still stand."

Branco rushed him, and Sean swung his sword to meet his attack. Steel clashing rang off the walls, and Sean grunted with surprise beneath Branco's powerful onslaught.

"Did you really think I would fight fair? I have the power of all that torture, all those deaths flowing through my body." Branco laughed in Sean's face as they tested each other.

"Yeah, well, you don't have the power of breath mints, buddy," Sean said in a low growling voice. He shifted his weight and ducked behind Branco.

Carmella turned her attention, ignoring everything now but the woman in front of her. Dianta was busy chanting a spell as Carmella approached. The words made her skin crawl. Dianta glared and smiled vindictively, her bright pink lipstick smeared across her teeth. With a scream, Dianta flung something at Carmella, and she easily dodged it. Time slowed down, and her body sped up, allowing her to see the green ball of energy well before it reached her. The energy hit the floor behind her and began to bubble and hiss in the decayed blood.

"Dianta Havel Mendez, daughter of Shyla Estrella Mendez, I come for you," Carmella said in a low voice that carried across the room louder than a scream.

The clash of blades of the two men fighting stopped, and Kell looked over from releasing

Tian's hand. Whatever Kell saw convinced him to move quicker. He grew pale, and his hands trembled as he undid the bindings.

Dianta yelled out, "You and what army, bitch? You're nothing. No one. And you can't hurt me. I'm a favorite of Guaricana." She backed away and held her hands up, but there was no energy left in her to hurl.

Shaking her head, Carmella stopped at the foot of the dais and stared at Dianta with a small, malicious smile. "I am the answer to a thousand whispered prayers. I am the righteous vengeance, and I am the hand of my god."

Dianta shrank back against the wall as Carmella closed on her. She stopped an arm's distance away, watching with disinterest as one of Dianta's false eyelashes came unglued and hung from her lid like a dead moth.

"Death is too quick for you. We want you to suffer," Carmella crooned as she stroked the hand holding the knife down Dianta's cheek. "What is inside will come out, and you will live an eternity of suffer with everyone able to see the filth that is your soul. You will pray for death a million times over but it will be denied to you until you've suffered ten times as much as your victims."

Dianta screamed in agony and tried to hit Carmella, who knocked her hand aside with a bone-breaking crunch. Dianta crumpled to the floor in a pile of fishnet and chains, sobbing and holding her shattered hand.

Carmella turned her back on Dianta and watched Kell hustle Tian out the door as gently as he could. The floor made a disgusting sucking sound as her shoes lifted across it, sticking to the tacky blood. From behind her came a long and hoarse scream as the curse began to give Dianta what she deserved. Carmella smiled and kept walking.

"Sean, we have to go," Carmella urged in a quiet voice, the ringing of swords blending in perfectly with its tone. She placed her hands over her ears, but kept her eyes open.

Sean lips moved as he sang, and even though Carmella couldn't hear it, she felt it in the pit of her stomach. The sensation was akin to sitting at the top of a roller coaster just about to make its decent.

Branco clutched his head and dropped to his knees while he shrieked in agony.

Sean sang, and Branco's hands trembled. His eyes rolled back to show only their whites, and his tongue swelled fat and purple, protruding past his lips. He slumped over, clawing at his throat, as dead as the men chained to the walls.

Carmella took a deep breath and smiled. With Bes using her, it was impossible to be upset. This was nothing compared to what the god had seen in his existence, and if he wasn't bothered, neither was Carmella.

"I will see you outside, my harmony." Sean placed a kiss on her cheek and hurried out the door.

Looking around the room, Carmella felt only pity and sadness. The souls of the men were still trapped here, being used as fuel for Guaricana's worshipers. She couldn't bring them back to life, but she could bring them peace.

Holy fire, Bes's voice whispered in her mind. It rang with the roar of a lion, the clashing of swords, and the gentle voice of a father.

Carmella looked around for Dianta, but she was gone. A trapdoor behind the dais stood open, leading into a dark tunnel. She must have escaped while Sean killed Branco. Carmella felt a moment of fear, but it was quickly swept away by the divine.

Unfamiliar words began to fall from her lips, heavy as stones and filled with power. The bodies of the dead men chained to the walls shivered as blue flames spread from their centers and licked up the walls. In her mind, her soul, she felt their grateful sighs as the spirits left their prison.

The fire didn't touch her, but it followed like a loyal dog as she made her way up the stairs and out of the bar. Her every step brought cleansing destruction.

Sean waited for her in the golden afternoon sunlight. He grabbed her into his arms as soon as she appeared. They both moved away from the doorway as it filled with smoke and blue flames. Running down the alley, they jumped into the waiting SUV. Kell drove them through the heavy traffic while Carmella sat on Sean's lap. Tian, laid out across the backseat, didn't make a sound.

Kell drove them into a park and stopped the SUV in an empty corner of the lot. Carmella yanked the door open and rushed to the backdoor. The wet ruin of Tian's back glistened in the sunlight with his small, short breaths. Carmella cried out and stroked his hair that was stiff with dried blood.

Sean took her hand away and replaced it with his own. "My god has some pretty neat tricks, too." She stepped back and let Kell hug her while they watched.

With the afternoon sunlight burning on their backs, Sean began to sing a gentle song. It was as soft as water running over stone, as soothing as a lullaby. Tian's back shimmered, and before Carmella's astonished eyes, it began to heal itself. Muscle knit over bone. Skin grew over exposed nerves.

Tian gave a mighty gasp and slumped back down onto the seat in a natural sleep. Kell closed the doors and hopped into the front seat with his cell phone glued to his ear.

Sean took Carmella into his arms and held her against the side of the SUV, smelling her hair. She held him close and rubbed her face against his shirt. The musky scent of his sweat mixed with the traces of his cologne. Her world had been turned upside down, but this perfect moment in Sean's arms brought her peace like she had never known.

His voice rumbled against her ear. "I promised to tell you what my harmony meant, didn't I?"

"Yes, you did." Carmella smiled, pulling back to look at Sean. He fitted so well in her arms.

"It means," he gave her a thorough kiss that filled her senses with joy, "that your soul is the perfect harmony for the melody of mine. We are meant to be together, our lives the perfect song." Too overcome by emotions for words, Carmella buried her hands in Sean's thick hair and pulled him in for a kiss that left them both pressed against each other, wanting more. With a reluctant sigh, Sean said, "We need to get going. I healed Tian, but he needs somewhere safe to sleep. Surrounded by love."

Carmella nodded and let out a deep breath. Bes's grace slipped away, but Sean's love filled the empty place it left behind perfectly.

Chapter Ten

Drums and music roared through the practice hall of the samba school. Sean shifted from foot to foot and tapped his fingers against his leather-clad thigh. Carnival was almost upon them, and he needed to get on to the massive winter-themed float that would follow the drum section of the samba school in the parade. A pair of black leather pants clung to his hips, and on his face he wore a complicated silver-and-blue ice mask, and that was about it. Sheer silver body paint glimmered on his skin, accenting the tattoo on his back.

Tian opened the door leading into the main part of the school. A hush came over the crowd as they waited for him to speak. He wore an elaborate white-and-neon-blue outfit, with white velvet pants that looked as though they were painted on. Tian grinned at Adam, his boyfriend, and blew him a kiss before turning serious. Tian's back had healed without a scar, and he didn't remember much of what had happened to him, thanks to Sean's magic and the healing power of Adam's love.

"Ladies and gentleman of the Ramirez Samba School, may I present to you your *Rainha da Bateria*...Carmella Ramirez!" Tian shouted as he led her out.

The crowd roared at a deafening volume while beating on their drums and playing their horns. Carmella wore the Snow Queen costume she had worked so hard on, and she looked spectacular. A few adjustments done by Sean's seamstress had altered the garment for her frame.

Long, white plumes of feathers spread out from her elaborate headdress, bits of blue sparkle catching the light. The feathers continued out in a halo to her shoulders, and the long plumes that attached to her back were spread out like angel's wings. Her golden skin shone without the need for paint or cosmetics. The elaborate snowflake pattern hugged Carmella's breasts, hinting at the bare skin beneath as they flowed down her hip and around one elegant leg.

The most beautiful thing of all to Sean's eyes was her smile. It was brilliant. Joy radiated from her as she wiped back a tear and continued to smile at the adoring crowd.

The people of the samba school were overjoyed that Miguel and Dianta had disappeared. A search of the office revealed that Miguel's father had left the school to

Carmella, with Miguel taking a role as a financial backer only. The lawyers were still going over it, but Carmella and her mother no longer had to worry about money. The dark shadow of evil had been lifted from the school. Hope and joy radiated from everyone who'd worked there for Carmella's father.

"You're drooling," Kell yelled into his ear over the noise.

Sean just grinned at him, and Kell laughed. Turning back to stare at Carmella, he felt for the small box in his pocket. He planned to ask her to marry him at the end of the parade. Two days ago, he had driven out to meet Carmella's mother, to ask for her blessing. It had been quickly given, and he bought her ring that day. It was a large central diamond, surrounded by smaller diamonds to look like a snowflake.

Carmella stalked over to him, her hips swinging, and the glittering snowflakes attached to her bikini bottom shimmered with each step. Sean stared, mesmerized by the contained sensuality. He might have a heart attack when she started to dance. Maybe he could get her to wear it on their honeymoon.

"Sean, I was thinking..." Carmella stroked a finger over her glittering cleavage.

"Uh-huh." Sean's gaze followed her finger, wishing it was his finger sliding over her amazing skin. His body burned whenever she was near. Everything about her drew him in—her kindness, her humor, her strength, and her obvious love for him. For the thousandth time, he sent a prayer of thanks for having her in his life.

Carmella snapped her fingers. "Up here, Sean. I was thinking about your offer to travel the world with you."

He held his breath and searched her face.

"I would love to."

Sean smiled and tried to keep his hand from straying to his pocket. It took all of his willpower to keep from proposing to her right now. If he did, they would both be useless for the Carnival. Not that he minded, but Carmella deserved her time in the sun as the Drum Queen. And he would be a sad man if he missed the sight of her dancing in that outfit to his music. "I would love it if you came with me, Carmella. I can't imagine not having you by my side."

"I was hoping you would say that." Carmella grasped his chin and tilted his head up. He had been admiring the white high heels with their long ribbons wrapping around her strong calves. "I already gave the job of manager of the school to Tian."

Sean glanced over her shoulder at Tian, who was busy doing last minute checks with all the dancers and musicians. "I take it he said yes?"

Carmella nodded, that brilliant smile back on her face. "I promised him we would stop by at least twice a year and always come back for Carnival."

Carefully, Sean stroked a hand down Carmella's cheek. "I would kiss you right now, but I think Tian would kill me for messing with your makeup."

Carmella's dark eyes filled with passion, and his leather pants were suddenly too tight. "After we are done tonight, you can wash this glitter off me, and I will wash that silver paint off you...and we'll make up for it."

Sean growled low in his throat and gently leaned in, brushing his lips softly over hers. "I love you."

Carmella's lips curved under his in a smile. "And I love you. Now, let's go see if your music can keep up with my hips."

****

Laughing, Sean carried Carmella over the threshold of the hotel room. To her immense satisfaction, a diamond engagement ring now glittered on her slender finger, marking her as his woman for everyone to see. Flipping on the low lights of the living room area of his suite, Sean barely ran his hands over her waist. A trail of goose bumps followed his touch, and she shivered.

"I'm glad you didn't propose to me until we were at the end of the parade," she murmured as he slid her down his body. The silver paint smeared and mixed with the sparkles on her skin.

"Why is that?" His strong and gentle fingers began to take out the dozens of pins and clips that held her headdress in place.

"Because I would have spent the rest of Carnival looking at my finger instead of dancing." The last pin came out, and she sighed as the headdress was lifted from her. As she tossed her shoes aside she admired the play of muscles while Sean carefully set the headdress on the coffee table.

"You're lucky you had any music to dance to. I thought I was going to lose my mind watching you move." His voice dipped to a base growl as he stalked across the room to her. "All that beautiful skin, sparkling in the lights. Knowing it was my beat moving you, my music bringing your body to life."

Suddenly unsure they were talking about music, her heart raced in her chest as he stopped right before her. One big hand cupped her cheek and moved down the side of her neck, pausing on one of the clasps holding her costume in place. He watched her carefully as he undid the clasp, making no move to remove the top.

The importance of this moment in her life had her close to shaking. Oh, she'd enjoyed the pleasures of the bed up to a certain point, but now she was more than ready to see everything that he had to offer. It was love that gave her the courage to undo the clasp on the back of her costume and slide the top down her shoulders.

The sharp inhalation of his breath as her breasts came into view heated her pussy and brought her nipples to hard points.

"So beautiful," he said in a low voice that stroked over her. He gently cupped her face and drew her in for a kiss. The tip of his tongue licked against her mouth, and she opened herself for him, drawing in the firm heat of his tongue.

Wrapping her arms around his back, she finally got to touch the firm ridges of muscle on either side of his spine, tracing her fingers down his silver skin to grab his butt. That broke a growl from him, and he pulled her closer, the firm length of his erection pressing into the softness of her belly.

Grinding against him, she tugged against the top of his pants, sliding her hands down to curve her hands around his bare ass. All of her hesitation was gone now, burned away by the feel of his body and the heat of his kiss.

"Shower." He groaned against her lips and stroked the sides of her breasts.

"What?" She pulled back and arched into his hands as they found her nipples, feather-light touches against the tips then a slightly rougher tug and pull. Each movement of his fingers had her pressing her hips into his and undulating until she was practically dancing against him.

"Shower," he said again, this time sounding a bit desperate.

A sharp tweak of her nipple had her shuddering. The world spun, and she squeaked as he threw her over his shoulder. "What are you doing?"

"Getting us into the shower before I lose my mind." He ran a hand over her costume-covered bottom. "Gods, I love your ass. It's so round and perfect. I want to eat it."

"Oh." She could hardly argue with that logic, or that erotic image.

Setting her down on the seat of the toilet, he turned on the multiple jets of the large shower and adjusted the water. Soon steam filled the air, and he turned to her. Tugging his boots and socks off, he moved closer to kneel in front of her.

"May I undress you?" he asked softly. The silver paint still shimmered on his shoulders, and his eyes were so dark now the blue was almost lost in the black of his pupils.

Nodding, she ran her hands through his hair, so soft and fine she would never grow tired of touching it. He pulled her to her feet and began to unclasp the bikini bottom, sliding it down her legs. Sitting back on his heels, he waited patiently for her to remove her hands from her mound.

She knew it was silly, but with him watching her so intently she had a sudden onset of shyness. Grinning at her, he stood and hooked his thumbs into the edge of his leather pants. Slowly, he drew them down over his hips, pausing to move them over the swell of his erection.

Her hands fell away at the sight of his rigid cock. Thick and full, a soft patch of darker red hair surrounded it. The girth made her eager to have him between her legs, and a low moan worked its way out of her throat as he stepped all the way out of his pants and stood naked before her.

Magnificent. Every inch of him was chiseled and carved muscle, from the heavy slabs of his thighs to the tight ridges of his stomach. His cock stood hard and proud, and she had to touch him. "Is that for me?" she whispered, suddenly bold and curious.

His answer choked off as she lightly wrapped her hand around him. Gods, he was big, and all hers. Using her nails, she lightly traced him from the base of his shaft to the tip. Big hands captured her face and brought her lips to his for a searing kiss that mimicked the stroking of her hand over his cock.

Pressing her against him, he lifted them both into the shower, never breaking the kiss. Warm water from the multiple jets poured over them, and the silver paint melted off his skin. The sensation of his suddenly slick skin beneath her hands had her pussy throbbing.

Breaking away, he grabbed a bar of soap and spun her around, placing her hands on the shower wall in front of her. Spreading her legs to brace herself, she moaned as his soapy hands worked over her shoulders and down the sides of her waist to her bottom.

"I have never seen such a perfect ass," he said and ran his hands over each mound, gripping her in an almost greedy fashion.

Her intended response faded to a groan as long fingers gently soaped the insides of her thighs, not touching her pussy but coming oh-so close. The water rushed over her, the feeling intensified by his touch. She sucked in a breath and trembled at the feeling of his tongue tracing over one butt cheek.

"Look at that pussy," he said with a sigh and rubbed his face on the back of her thigh. "So swollen and wet." Turning her hips gently, he spun her around and widened her stance.

Gripping his wet hair, she urged his mouth to her mound, and he complied. Hot and soft, his tongue spread the folds of her labia and gently sucked at the soft inner lips. The sensation had her kneading her fingers in his hair, groaning her need as he worked her. His own groan joined hers as he spread the top of her labia, exposing her clit.

A delicate stroke of the tongue over that stiff nub had her stumbling against the shower. Instead of releasing her, he threw one of her legs over his shoulder and sucked hard. Pleasure, intense and hot, ripped through her body, and she arched into him. He gently bit her clit and held it between his teeth while his tongue lashed over the tip, driving her arousal higher until she was mindless with need. Long and hard, each suck brought her closer to her orgasm.

Rocking her hips to his face in time with his sucks, she cupped her breasts and pulled on her nipples. This was Sean bringing her pleasure, Sean feasting on her as if she were the most delicious thing he had ever tasted. Hunching over, her body tensed and trembled on the edge. His low growl vibrated through her body and tipped her over the edge.

So good, the orgasm snapped her hips against his mouth and had her screaming. Wave after wave of bliss racked her body until she struggled to get away from his mouth. It was too much, too intense. With a final lick, so soft it was barely a touch, he released her and stared up at her through the water.

"You taste like passion," he growled out, and she shivered.

He stood and slammed the handle, turning the water off and leaving her shivering. Tugging her out after him, he tossed a towel around her and picked her up. Wrapping her legs around his waist, she marveled at his strength as he carried her. The muscles of his stomach moved against her sensitive pussy, stirring to life the passion that seemed so close to the surface around him.

They fell onto the bed together, a tangle of wet hair and damp limbs. Reaching down between them, she spread the moisture over the head of his cock and gave him a rough squeeze. His answering groan rumbled through her body, and she twisted beneath the magic of his voice. It carried its own enchantment and stroked against her soul.

Sliding up farther, his chest hair dragged against her breasts, and the tip of his cock rested against her entrance. Taking a deep breath, he hesitated and looked into her eyes. "I love you." With that, the head of his cock pushed past the thin membrane of her maidenhead and began to ease into her. There was a moment of pain, but it was more the adjustment to his size than anything else.

Slowly, with delicious control, he pressed himself into her. His eyes closed, and she watched him, as turned on by the expression of deep pleasure on his face as his cock moving within her. At last he sank all the way to the base of his shaft and held still within her.

Burying his face in her hair, he held her close and began to move just the slightest bit. The sensation tore the breath from her lungs, and she kissed the side of his neck, wiggling her hips beneath him. Taking the hint, his moves became more forceful, long strokes that left her gasping.

"Sean," she purred out and snapped her hips to meet his. Their bellies met with harsh claps as he lifted up onto his forearms and looked down between them. Following the line of his gaze, she groaned at the sight of his flushed cock thrusting into her welcoming heat.

The tension began to build again, and she ran her hands over his chest, his body slick with his sweat and the moisture from their shower. He did something with his hips that had her grabbing on to his shoulders and begging him not to stop. Each thrust, each feeling of the head of his cock pulling almost all the way out only to rush back in, pushed her closer.

"Can't hold back," he groaned out, and that gave her the edge she needed to come again. Holding on to him so hard it hurt, she relished the totally new and fantastic feeling of coming with a cock buried deep inside of her. The delicate inner muscles of her pussy grabbed on to him and new nerve endings sent wave after wave of bliss through her until she was screaming beneath him.

He growled out something in a language she didn't understand and threw his head back, his body shuddering as he emptied himself into her. Coasting down from her own orgasm, she could feel the hot spurts of his seed filling her then trickling out as he strained and whispered her name.

Panting, he rolled her over onto his chest, still inside of her. As the endorphins faded, a slight ache began to make itself known, and she gently moved him out of her with a wince.

"Are you okay?" he asked, brushing her hair back from her face.

Laughing, she grabbed the towel and tenderly cleaned herself. A small trace of red appeared on the towel, and she blushed and tossed it to the side. "I am more than okay." She rubbed her face on his chest, licking at his nipple. "That was, that was … amazing."

A smug smile curved his lips, and he stretched his arms out behind his head. "Thank you."

After rolling her eyes, she explored his body at a leisurely pace. He sighed in contentment as her fingers traced over his chest and up to his mouth. Nipping one of her fingers, he pulled it in and sucked at the tip.

Watching him with half-lidded eyes, she smiled as he released her finger and kissed the engagement ring. "Sean, what exactly does it mean to be your harmony?"

"Your soul is the perfect harmony to my soul's melody." He smoothed his hand down her back, pausing to trace a fingertip over the indentation of her spine. "We were meant to be together, destined to love one another and to live happily ever after."

She couldn't help but smile at him and say in a teasing voice, "So we are going to make beautiful music together?"

Rich and decadent, his chuckle made her toes curl against the sheets. "Well, you do make the most wonderful sounds when you're aroused." His mouth found her nipple and sucked it into a hard, aching bud. "Let's see if I can make you sing again."

Relaxing in his embrace, Carmella said a prayer of thanks to Bes for bringing Sean into her life. A warm flash of divine love raced through her soul, and she lost herself in Sean's touch.

The End

Coming next in The Chosen series: Blessed

A Thank you from Fated Desires

Thank you so much for reading **Cursed**! We're so happy that you had a chance to look into the fantasy world of The Chosen. We do hope if you liked this, that you would please leave a review from where you purchased this or on another platform. Not only does a review spread the word to other readers, they let us know if you'd like to see more stories like this from us. Ann loves to hear from readers and talks to them when she can. You can reach her through her website and through her Facebook and Twitter accounts. You guys are the reason we get to do what we do and we thank you.

If you are looking for more stories like these, you don't have to wait much longer! Ann is cooking up new works in this series and a few others. Also, we have a few new authors coming that will be sure to whet your appetite.

If you'd like to know more about Fated Desires, check out our website or email us at admin@FatedDesires.com.

About the Author

With over thirty published books, Ann is Queen of the Castle to her wonderful husband and three sons in the mountains of West Virginia. In her past lives she's been an Import Broker, a Communications Specialist, a US Navy Civilian Contractor, a Bartender/Waitress, and an actor at the Michigan Renaissance Festival. She also spent a summer touring with the Grateful Dead- though she will deny to her children that it ever happened.

From a young age she's been fascinated by myths and fairytales, and the romance that was often the center of the story. As Ann grew older and her hormones kicked in, she discovered trashy romance novels. Great at first, but she soon grew tired of the endless stories with a big wonderful emotional buildup to really short and crappy sex. Never a big fan of purple prose, throbbing spears of fleshy pleasure and wet honey pots make her giggle, she sought out books that gave the sex scenes in the story just as much detail and plot as everything else- without using cringe worthy euphemisms. This led her to the wonderful world of Erotic Romance, and she's never looked back.

Now Ann spends her days trying to tune out cartoons playing in the background to get into her 'sexy space' and has accepted that her Muse has a severe case of ADD.

Ann loves to talk with her fans, as long as they realize she's weird and that sarcasm doesn't translate well via text.

Also from this Author

Now Available

Submissive's Wish
Ivan's Captive Submissive

The Chosen
Cursed

Virtual Seduction
Sodom and Detroit
Sodom and the Phoenix

Prides of the Moon
Amber Moon
Emerald Moon
Turquoise Moon
Amethyst Moon
Onyx Moon
Opal Moon
Prides of the Moon

For the Love of Evil
Daughter of Lust
Princess of Lust

Ultimate Fantasy
Scandalous Wish
Pursued by the Prisoner

Club Wicked
My Wicked Valentine
My Wicked Nanny
My Wicked Devil
My Wicked Trainers

Sam and Cody
Want
Cherish
Adore

Other Titles
Blushing Violet
Wild Lilly
The Breaker's Concubine
Peppermint Passion
The Bodyguards Princess
Diamond Heart
Sensation Play
Summer's Need
Still
Guarding Hope

Coming Soon

The Chosen
Blessed
Dreamer

Did you enjoy this selection? Why not try another romance from Fated Desires?

From Ann Mayburn's Submissive's Wish series:

Ivan's Captive Submissive

Chapter One

Gia Lopez stood in a staging area for the submissive auction with a line of women covered in sheer black robes. Her long, light brown hair was twisted back into an intricate braid that was a work of art, but she desperately wished she'd gotten plastic surgery to take care of her big nose before agreeing to this. The other women scheduled to be sold off with her were beautiful, each perfect and lovely in their own way.

She felt like a sparrow surrounded by peacocks.

While Gia possessed enough self-worth to admit she was cute with her dimples and big brown eyes, she'd never be breathtaking like the auburn haired sex-bomb submissive next to her. Gia had a slender figure from her daily jogging, but with her small breasts she felt like a boy when compared with the curvy submissive.

Why couldn't Gia have gone after someone who wasn't a pinup girl?

Mistress Alice, a tall, blonde Domme, walked down the line of submissives. They were gathered in what looked like parlor with all the furniture moved out. Elegant watercolors still graced the walls and a tasteful chandelier bathed the room in a low, golden light. The door to the room where the auction would take place was currently closed, but from her orientation earlier, Gia knew that on the other side there was a curtained area to hide them from the audience. Then, the scariest of all, a stage where she would be sold to the highest bidder.

Mistress Alice paused now and again to point out something she wanted changed with a submissive's hair or makeup and took a moment to speak with each woman. Up at the front of the line, a few men in brown leather loincloths presented a nice visual treat as they were oiled up by a trio of giggling submissives.

Mistress Alice stopped before Gia and slowly inspected her from head to toe. When she spotted the gold barbells piercing Gia's nipples through the sheer cloth of the gown, she smiled. "Lovely touch against your nicely tanned skin. The gold works much better than silver."

"Thank you, Mistress Alice." Gia curtsied as she'd been trained and Mistress Alice's gaze warmed.

The Domme tilted her head and studied Gia's face. "You're Mistress Viola and Master Mark's girl from South Carolina, Gia."

"Yes, Ma'am. Mistress Viola and Master Mark were my trainers."

"Lovely couple. I met them once at a Domme convention in Las Vegas. They told me to keep an eye on you, that you have quite a temper and are very high spirited."

Gia flushed and dropped her gaze. "I'm working on that, Mistress Alice."

"Well don't work on it too hard." She leaned closer and whispered, "Some of us like a subs with fire in their veins. We like the challenge and the constant battle for your submission."

Gia started as the other woman gently bit her earlobe before leaning back. "Am I understood?"

A soft rush of desire went through Gia and she licked her lower lip. "Yes, Mistress."

The desire unfurled gently in her belly as she relived her training and how she owed her trainers a debt she could never repay. It had been a unique experience to work with Mistress Viola and Master Mark. Together they'd helped her start her transformation into the kind of submissive she yearned to be. They'd also given her glorious orgasms that swept the world away and left her existing as a being of pure pleasure. Not only did they train her physically, they helped her learn how to love herself just the way she was.

Mistress Viola was a plump, curvy, delicious armful of woman. By today's standards she was considered overweight, but back in the 1950's she would have been the ultimate in female beauty. Gia had yet to see a man who didn't gravitate to Mistress Viola in a room, no matter how many other women were there. The fact that her husband, the more traditionally handsome Master Mark, loved her beyond reason helped more than anything else to make Gia believe that maybe there was a man out there that could love her just as she was and give her the confidence to become the woman she wanted to be.

Beautiful, elegant, and loved.

Well, she wasn't loved yet, but she would be. She had faith her Master was out there, looking for her. The thought of him being here tonight, maybe waiting for her in the audience, sent an ache of longing through her. The practical part of her mind scoffed at the idea of soul mates and fate, but the romantic side of her nature insisted anything was possible.

A petite mahogany-skinned woman who reminded Gia of a pixie came up to Mistress Alice and knelt at her feet. "Mistress, Master Martin wishes me to inform you we have fifteen minutes until we begin."

Mistress Alice nodded. "Thank you, Tilly." She smiled at Gia, "Have fun, sweet girl. Whoever gets you is going to have their hands full."

"Thank you, Mistress." Gia bent into a graceful curtsey.

The pair went farther down the line and Gia tried to slow her breathing. The redhead in front of Gia turned around and gave her a warm and dazzling smile. "First time?"

"Yes. Is it painfully obvious?"

"Yep. First timers are pretty easy to spot. You're the only ones who aren't excited. My name is Iris."

"Gia. Nice to meet you." Gia smiled and smoothed her hands against the sheer robe. "I take it by your lack of panic attacks you've done this before?"

"Oh, yes. This is my third time." Iris gave a dreamy smile. "After the first auction, I was bought by a lovely Dominant couple. At the second auction, I met my husband, who is also my Master."

Gia tilted her head in confusion. As far as she knew, this auction was for single, uncollared submissives. "If you have a Master, why are you doing this again?"

The woman laughed and fingered her collar. "Because he wants to win me all over again."

Gia couldn't help a small stab of envy. "That's very romantic."

A chime sounded three times, silencing all conversation. All of the submissives turned towards the sound, and the redhead leaned over to whisper into Gia's ear, "Don't freak out. Whoever you end up with is going to be one of the best Masters in the world. If you click, great. If you don't, then you will, at the very least, come away from the experience as a better submissive. Besides, all of the Masters have your fantasies available to them, and only a Master or Mistress interested in fulfilling your fantasies will bid on you."

Gia laced her fingers together, trying to keep her anxiety at bay. She didn't want to start shaking like a scared puppy. "That's what worries me." She lowered her voice and leaned closer to Iris. "I shared a bottle of wine, or two, with my girlfriend before I filled my form out, and I'm afraid the fantasies I submitted are a little more...frank. Let's just say I was super honest about what my deepest, darkest desires are. Like, embarrassingly honest. When I read what I had already submitted the next morning, I couldn't look myself in the mirror for the rest of the day without feeling like a pervert."

Iris giggled. "Oh, that does sound interesting. Care to share what one of those fantasies were?"

A stern man's voice range out over the crowd. "Ladies, eyes on me."

They turned and Gia recognized Master Martin, the man who ran the Submissive's Wish Charity Auction and owner of this elegant mansion. Tonight, the distinguished man wore a dashing black tux with an expertly tied red and black bowtie that nicely set off his greying hair. His presence filled the room and all conversation stopped.

Raising his arms, he smiled. "Welcome to the twenty eighth annual Submissive's Wish Charity Auction. Some of your faces are well known to me as members, and others are delightful new additions to our evening.

Whether new or old, I encourage all of you to make the most of the opportunities presented to you tonight. Allow yourselves to embrace your submission and give yourselves the freedom to enjoy the fantasies your Masters or Mistresses create for you without useless shame or misplaced guilt. For the next week, you will be at your Masters' or Mistresses' beck and call. You will find yourself challenged, pushed beyond what you thought you could endure but, in the end, it will all be worth it."

A nervous giggle came from a few of the submissives and Master Martin smiled, then his expression turned serious again. "Let me take this opportunity to emphasize once again that your happiness is the most important part of this auction. If you are purchased by someone that you do not wish to have sexual relations with you are by no means obligated to do so. The only thing the Master or Mistress that win's you gets is your company. It is up to them to try to seduce you and make you fall under their wicked spell."

Barely stifling a wistful sigh, Gia wondered if she was really ready for this. Yes, she'd submitted to Mistress Viola and Master Mark while training, but she'd never managed to achieve subspace. After listening enviously to the way the other submissives talked about it, she really wanted to experience it but, truthfully, didn't know if she could. She'd tried with a couple of local Doms that she was friendly with back home in Myrtle Beach. While the sex had been great, she'd never even gotten close to achieving that floaty, orgasmic feeling the other submissives described. It made her feel like a failure as a submissive that she couldn't get into the right headspace for her Dominants.

Hell, if whoever won her here couldn't top her, maybe she should consider becoming a Domme.

Master Martin's deep voice interrupted her dark thoughts. "You will soon be blindfolded and ear buds will be put into your ears so you cannot hear. We want you to focus on yourself, on your goals, on what you hope to gain from this experience. Not on what is happening around you."

Gia shifted nervously and the air around her became charged and crackled with tense energy.

"Don't worry about how you'll walk or move around while blindfolded. You will each be escorted onto stage by an experienced submissive." He looked up and down the line. "Any questions? No? Such a quiet and trusting group of submissives we have here tonight."

Everyone chuckled, then a curvaceous dark skinned Dominatrix towards the back of the line raised her hand. "Master Martin?"

Master Martin smiled. "Our lovely Mistress Vivienne. What is your question?"

Mistress Vivienne smiled. "This girl," she pointed to the petite woman with a riot cute dark curls in front of her, "is worried she may end up with some serial killer."

The submissive flushed beet red and seemed to sink in on herself. Gia felt sorry for her, but she'd been wondering about that as well. Of course, this auction had been running for twenty-eight years without incident, and everyone had been highly screened, but all it took was one bad apple to end her life. Great. Now she was nervous and scared. It seemed like her brain would never turn all the way off and let her relax.

She liked being in control of her life, leaving nothing to chance or fate, but being constantly on her guard was mentally and emotionally draining. She hated not having control over what was happening to her, which was probably why she had such a hard time submitting. It took trust in the unknown to let someone truly inside your mind and heart during a scene and to totally let go. So far, no one had managed to breech the walls around her soul. That was fine, she was in no hurry to get serious...though it would be nice to have someone to cuddle with at night and wake up to in the morning. Someone to share holidays with and someone who would not only satisfy her physically, but also intellectually. She thought about being in some faceless man's arms as they watched the sunrise over the Atlantic ocean together and let out a sigh.

Master Martin cleared his throat and her attention returned to him. "As we have a larger than usual number of visiting submissives for this auction, I will reiterate what our members already know. There is not a single Master or

Mistress out in the audience tonight I wouldn't trust my own submissive with....though I doubt any of them could actually handle Mrs. Martin." He waited for the polite laughter to die down before continuing. "Every single one of our bidders has gone through extensive background checks and have been members in high standing of their local clubs for a minimum of five years. While nothing in life is ever guaranteed, I take the safety of every man and woman here very seriously. Does that answer your question, darling girl?"

The blushing woman dipped into an elegant curtsey and said in a lightly accented voice, "Yes, Sir. Thank you, Master Martin."

"You are most welcome. Anymore questions?"

"Sir?" A willowy woman with short blonde hair held her hand up.

"Yes."

"Will I have access to my luggage at all times? I'm a diabetic and will need to be able to get to my medication."

"Of course. The suitcase we asked you to bring has all of your important identification, including your passports, and medication inside along with a change of clothes. We've also included two thousand dollars, cash. If you feel uncomfortable and you'd like to leave you can do so without having to rely on anyone to help you." An uneasy murmur went through the submissives and he gave them a bemused smile. "We haven't had a single submissive leave before their time was up, but we like to make sure that you feel as comfortable as possible."

"Any other last minute questions?"

Silence blanketed the room and Gia laced her fingers together again. Her background check had taken six months. By the time it was done, they knew everything about her—from who her best friend had been in elementary school to her preferences in food. She hoped the Dominants had to go through background checks as thorough. This whole experience was so outside her comfort zone that it was quickly turning into something surreal, like a confusing dream where the scenes changed too quickly to really get a grasp on what was happening.

If it wasn't for the fact the money raised from her auction would go directly to her charity of choice, she'd be tempted to pretend to be sick and run as far and as fast as she could. Then she'd probably spend the rest of her life kicking herself in the ass for missing the opportunity to serve a true Master, however temporarily. No, she wasn't going to chicken out. She wasn't quitter and she certainly wasn't going to let her fear rule her now. Though the thought of hiding in a bathroom with a fifth of tequila to gain some liquid courage seemed like a great idea.

She was such a basket case.

When no one spoke up, Mr. Martin gestured toward the back of the room. "Let me introduce you to the men and women who will help you navigate the stage."

Laughter rang from the doorway at the back of the room, and a steady stream of elegantly dressed men and women came to stand before them. A lovely Latina wearing a golden cat mask that matched her elaborate gown stopped before Gia with a friendly smile. Taking a closer look at the gown, Gia was pretty sure she'd seen it on the cover of this month's edition of *Vogue*. A diamond collar with a small gold owner's medallion glittered around her slender neck.

"Good evening. My name is Harper and I'll be taking care of you, Gia."

Giving the other woman a tentative smile, Gia almost held out her hand in the traditional 'nice to meet you' handshake but remembered where she was and who she was with. While shaking hands might be the proper thing to do in the outside world, the BDSM community had its own rules on what was proper. In this case, she didn't know if Harper was allowed to touch another submissive without her Master's permission. Gathering herself, she smiled back.

"Thank you. If I throw up on you or pass out, I apologize in advance." Gia flushed in embarrassment at how uncouth she sounded compared to this elegant and sophisticated woman.

Harper giggled and pulled a black blindfold out of her elbow length white silk gloves. "I'll make sure to aim you in the other direction at all times. Now take a deep breath before you pass out." Gia did as she was told and took another, which seemed to help clear her head.

The tall female submissive attending the redhead next to Gia smiled at Harper. "Did you hear? The European delegation is in the audience tonight. Yummy."

Gia blinked. "The Europeans?"

Lifting the blindfold, Harper smiled. "Bend down a bit so I can tie this."

The cool cloth slipped loosely over her eyes and the other woman said, "The Europeans are here as part of a...well kind of like a cultural exchange program. They send their top Dommes and Masters over here for training and we send our best Dommes and Masters over there for the same thing. I've heard they're strict, but amazing."

"And they are soooo hot," Iris said with a purr. "I love my Master more than anything in the world, but if I was single I'd be begging any one of them to take me like the willing slut that I am."

All three women laughed, then hushed when Master Martin looked their way a raised brow.

Harper adjusted the blindfold until Gia couldn't see anything and said in a softer voice, "Okay, the ear buds are going back in. I can tell you from experience, once they're on, you won't be able to hear anything. I'm going to hold your hand the whole time so, if you start to get a little anxious, just give me a squeeze. Got it?"

"Yes, ma'am, I mean Harper."

The beautiful woman's laughter was the last thing Gia heard before Harper placed some ear buds in her hand and Gia put them in her ears.

A gentle, classical piece of music played from the tiny speakers, but the soothing melody did nothing to calm her nerves. Feeling suddenly very alone and vulnerable, a wave of distress tightened her muscles and she reached out. Almost instantly, Harper's hand grasped hers, the smooth satin of Harper's glove giving Gia something to focus on. No wonder men liked the feeling of a woman wearing gloves. It somehow accentuated how much smaller a woman was, how finely formed.

Harper squeezed her hand twice and began to lead Gia forward then stopped again. With the ear buds in place, Gia couldn't have a conversation with the other woman and was left with her own thoughts. Once again, they moved forward, and then stopped. By Gia's estimate, each time they paused they waited a good five to ten minutes. She should be using this time to think, to compose herself so she presented the best image possible. After all, she only had one chance to make a positive first impression on some of the best Dominants in the world. Unfortunately, her mind refused to stay on one topic for more than a few seconds.

Her thoughts were chaotic, jumping from concern about her appearance to wondering if she needed a breath mint. A fine tremor went through her hands and she worried that she'd be shaking like a frightened animal on the stage. Mixed in with that was the reoccurring fear that she'd sweat through her deodorant before they made it through the door and that she had some toilet paper stuck to her sheer robe. Opening herself to the potential, very public rejection of nobody bidding on her was so far out of her comfort zone that she didn't know how to cope with her rising panic. This was like stage fright times a million.

Someone removed one of the ear buds and Harper whispered, "We're going up on the stage now to wait. You look beautiful, and I have no doubt there will be a bidding war for you." She put the ear bud back in and Gia was left alone with her spazztic thoughts and the mellow strains of a violin concerto.

Harper gave Gia's hand a tight squeeze and led her slowly up a ramp. The carpet beneath her feet changed to a smooth, cool surface and she realized she was now on the stage. At least her big feet looked cute. As part of her welcome package to the auction she had a full spa treatment consisting of dozens of feminine indulgences she'd never experienced before, including a pedicure that left her with pretty rose pink toenails, and baby soft feet. Spending that kind of money on pampering herself wasn't in her Ramen noodle budget so she'd enjoyed the experience immensely. Every hair-free inch of her body below the neck had been polished until it gleamed like bronze.

She almost licked her lips, then remembered the Domme who had expertly done her makeup had threatened to flog her if she messed up her glossy pale red lipstick. Gia was to be perfect, and that meant controlling herself for the pleasure of the crowd as she stood on stage at the auction. Right now though, she was about to pass out from fear despite Harper's sure grip. They stood still, and the occasional brush of air from someone passing would tingle over Gia's overly sensitive skin. With her sight and hearing taken away she became hyper aware of any stimulation around her.

The idea of doing the charity submissive auction had seemed like a dream come true at first. Gia had a low paying job as an architect with long hours and asshole clients. In this economy, she was lucky to have gained legitimate employment with health benefits anywhere after she graduated. True, her work only paid her enough to give her a roof over her head and other basic necessities, but she knew if she busted her ass, she could and would rise through the corporate ranks. Unfortunately, all that work resulted in a miserable lack of a social life and an even more abysmal love life. Yes, she played at her local club, but it was more physical than emotional. She always left feeling that there had to be more to BDSM than what she'd experienced.

When the Submissive's Wish Charity Auction came up, she'd jumped at the chance. If a Dominant bought her, the money would go to the charity of Gia's choice, and she would get ten percent of whatever was bid. Gia planned on using the extra money she made to put a down payment on a house. She was tired of living in an apartment complex where people fought or partied at all hours of the night. The thought of being able to sleep without being awakened by the sound of techno or Fanny's screaming because she caught Joe cheating again was heaven.

She already knew where she wanted to buy some land with access to the ocean so she could build her dream home someday. The money from the auction could make that happen years ahead of schedule. First, she had to appeal to someone enough to be bid on. When she'd first applied for the Submissive's Wish Charity Auction they told her some of the submissives offered never got bid on, and she shouldn't take it personally if it happened to her. She couldn't imagine how humiliating that would be and prayed someone would find her lean frame, bubble butt and exotic looks appealing enough to make up for her lack of experience.

Gia stood with her back straight, her shoulders gracefully curved, and one leg slightly in front of the other, turning her body to a subtle angle. Mistress Viola had pointed out how it showed off Gia's long legs and big, round ass. At the time, Gia wasn't sure if she was offended or flattered, but now she tried to accept her bubble butt as part of the way God made her.

Taking in a deep breath, she slowly let it out and tried to focus on the positive. She'd beaten incredible odds to make it this far, so there had to be something inside her the Auction Committee found appealing. Hell, she hoped she was attracted to whoever won her. She liked big, strong men and the sight of a pair of broad shoulders and narrow waist always made her heart beat harder. With her luck, she'd be bid on and won for ten bucks by a skinny guy with dandruff.

A soft, satin glove-covered hand touched Gia's chin and brought her back to the present with a rush of nerves. Gia let out a soft moan. It must be her turn. The ear buds were removed, and a moment later, the blindfold was taken from her eyes.

Harper stood in front of her with a warm smile curving her full lips. She looked like a golden goddess while Gia felt like a walking plague victim.

God, please let at least one person bid on her.

Just one.

Leaning forward, Harper whispered, "Breathe."

Gia sucked in a deep lungful of air and immediately felt better, less faint. Harper gave her a moment, then gracefully helped Gia walk to the center of the stage. They were in what had to be a ballroom, lit so she couldn't see anything about the crowd. It was just she and Harper standing in a pool of warm light while an anonymous group of people inspected her from the shadows.

Harper held Gia's hand out and cleared her throat. Flushing, Gia remembered to curtsey to the audience. A soft chuckle flowed through the crowd, and she blushed so hot even her ears burned. Obviously, they hadn't missed her chagrined look.

A male voice filled the auditorium.

"Masters and Mistresses, may I present Gia. Joining us from South Carolina, she holds a master's degree in architecture and is relatively new to the lifestyle. Her charity of choice is a no-kill animal shelter in Myrtle Beach where she has volunteered for the past three years. While she has been trained by the esteemed Mistress Viola and Master Mark on the basics of submission, she has much to learn. I've heard she's a very eager student. We've also been warned she has a temper, so it will take a strong Master or Mistress to win her submission."

The crowd laughed, and the murmurs through the audience grew louder. Gia flushed hot enough to melt the sun. She'd imagined she'd get up here, the guy would point out that she had nice legs in spite of her chunky butt and she liked to give blowjobs.

Oh shit, were they going to talk about the sexual fantasies she'd written down for them? She thought they were going to be in the program next to a picture of her or something, not actually talked about while she stood here. Anxiety tightened her muscles and she worried people in the audience could see her hands trembling.

God, they were going to think she was a weirdo, a pervert, a freak, all those things she secretly felt about herself. No, she wouldn't give into those negative thoughts. Mistress Viola had spent a great deal of time talking with Gia about her sexual needs. The one thing Mistress emphasized above all else was that

Gia should be honest with her partner and herself about what her needs were, and not be ashamed of her natural desires. The mature woman part of her mind agreed, while the prim and proper portion insisted she was a sexual deviant and needed therapy.

Sure enough, the next words that rolled out of the auctioneer's mouth made her wince. "Gia is fond of forced seduction and abduction scenarios. She also enjoys relationships where the man is powerful, someone to be feared and respected, but gentle with her...to a point. She craves dominance and has yet to achieve subspace. Well, I'm sure we can help her learn how to fly."

More audience laughter, along with a few catcalls. "Her trainers, Mistress Viola and Master Mark from the South Carolina club, The Iron Fist, have said she can be a bit of a brat and will need a firm hand. At her core, Gia is eager to please and wants to be found worthy of your attentions."

Harper gave her fingers the barest squeeze and whispered, "Breathe."

Gia sucked in an audible breath, and the audience chuckled. She imagined how they were talking about her, commenting on her bony knees, her giraffe neck, her tiny breasts. Here, under the bright lights, all of her insecurities threatened to rise to the surface and overwhelm her. A man to the left commented on her pierced nipples while a woman somewhere ahead of her made a nasty remark about Gia's small tits.

This was the single most embarrassing, humiliating, terrible experience of her life. Tears threatened to fill her eyes and she blinked rapidly. No, she was not going to cry, at least, not right now. When no one bid on her, she could let her tears flow.

"This lovely submissive has agreed to one week serving the winning bidder. Masters and Mistresses, let us start the bidding at one hundred thousand dollars."

Gia swallowed hard as the first bid came in. She had no idea how the auctioneer could see who was in the audience, but the bids kept climbing. When the staggering figure of close to four hundred thousand dollars was reached she openly gaped.

Two men were bidding. One was an American from one of the New England states by his cultured tone. The other had a rough, almost bestial voice with a sharp, growling tenor to it and an accent she couldn't place. Her few remaining brain cells that weren't freaking out, tried to focus on the spot the voices were coming from. She could barely see the outline of what might be people sitting in chairs.

The man with the rough, accented voice roared out, "Four hundred and twenty-five thousand dollars."

Silence hung heavy in the air. Even the auctioneer seemed stunned. It took him a moment to respond before he coughed and said, "I have four hundred and twenty-five thousand US dollars. Going once...going twice...sold!"

Gia stood there in total shock. Four hundred and twenty-five thousand dollars! That was a life-changing amount of money for the rescue shelter. She spent one weekend a month volunteering, so she knew exactly how far they could stretch it—definitely a new building, maybe even enough to purchase the plot of land behind them and turn it into a dog run. They could even add a full-time vet on staff with that kind of money.

With a gentle tug, Harper brought Gia's thoughts back to the present in a rush. Harper smiled at her and led her to the edge of the stage. Her time with the winning bidder began right now. For the amount he paid for her, Gia wanted to show him the time of his life, to somehow be worth all the money he'd spent. Hell, she didn't care if he was eighty years old with liver spots on his balls, she would do her best to rock his world in thanks for his amazingly generous bid.

The spotlights turned away and she blinked rapidly, trying to adjust her eyesight. They took a few steps and were almost at the main floor when Harper paused. A moment passed, then a man said something in what she thought was Russian or some type of Slavic language. She looked to Harper, who gave her a slight shake of her head. Great. Harper didn't understand what was going on either.

A second man approached and she could see him a bit better. His suit was tan and stood out in the dim lighting of the audience.

"Your new Master extends his greeting. He is pleased to have won your service. You will wait for him in one of the sitting rooms while he finishes his business here."

Gia took a deep breath. Okay, she was really doing this. Soon she was going to make her first impression with a Master, not just any Master, *her* Master. She needed to do this right, but she really wished she could see what he looked like.

She held her hand out and the man in the tan suit moved forward. He helped her down from the stage and released her once she reached the bottom. He motioned to her, and she followed him out of the auditorium past men and women whose attention had returned to the stage where the next submissive was being brought out. They went down an elegantly appointed hallway done in red tones until he stopped before a door with the number seven on it. He opened the door and held it for her.

"Please wait inside. He will be with you soon."

She wanted to ask who 'he' was, but silence seemed to be the best option at this point.

The man in the tan suit left quickly, and she turned to look at the room around her. To her surprise it wasn't some kinky sex room, but rather a small reading area. A fire crackled in the black marble hearth, and deep burgundy velvet chairs were arranged artfully before it. Books lined the walls, but she didn't think she could focus enough to read.

There was a gilt-framed mirror above the fireplace, so she took a moment to check her reflection. A few wisps of her wavy light brown hair had escaped her waist length braid and she quickly smoothed them back into place. Her makeup was intact, and she did a quick check of her breath. Good to go there as well.

Not knowing what else to do, she knelt in the center of the room and waited for her Master as she'd been taught.

She'd scarcely settled and arranged her robe about her in what she hoped was a pleasing manner when the door handle turned again. It opened revealing a massive, thoroughly intimidating man with dark hair that was cut so close on the sides it was almost shaved. A scar went down his cheek and bisected his lips before trailing down to his strong chin. He wore an impeccably tailored, black wool suit that highlighted his fit figure. On his wrist gleamed a gold watch that probably cost more than her apartment building.

She'd been expecting some elegant, sophisticated man who reeked money and class. The man standing before her was plain scary. Despite his obviously high-end apparel he somehow exuded danger. In a way, he reminded her of the proverbial wolf in sheep's clothing. He was a good five inches taller than she with a body like a prizefighter. No pretty gym muscles here; this man had a barrel chest and massive thighs, not to mention huge arms.

Gia looked back to his face and forced herself to meet his brilliant blue eyes. To her surprise he had the prettiest eyes she'd ever seen, Caribbean blue with hints of green here and there. They seemed out of place in his rough and imposing features. He had a solid jaw, good cheekbones, and a nose that was a little bit bigger than normal and looked like it had been broken more than once.

The man reached down and took her hand. As he pulled her to her feet, she had the impression of great strength. The hand holding hers was large with scars across the knuckles. Whoever this man was, he'd been a fighter at one time. The scent of his cologne reached her and she took in a greedy lungful of the air around him. He smelled delicious, like leather and spice.

"My name is Ivan. I am your new Master's bodyguard, and I will be taking you to him."

His voice was a deep rumble, like rocks grinding against each other. She was surprised to find herself disappointed he wasn't the man who had bought her. Attraction arced between them and she looked away, embarrassed by her body's reaction to the man who was not her new Master.

Unable to help herself, she took another deep breath of his cologne and her overactive imagination began to conjure all kinds of kinky things. Glancing down at his big hands she tried to imagine what it would be like to be spanked by someone as large as him, or what it would feel like to have all of that weight on her, pushing her into the mattress while he fucked her. Power and strength radiated from him in a way she'd never experienced with any Dom before, similar to the way Master Martin's presence filled the room but somehow... sharper.

Her nipples drew to hard points and she quickly looked away from him. She'd always had a thing for men's hands and his were inspiring an almost dizzying amount of lust. He moved his hands so they framed his crotch, and she realized with a start he thought she was staring at his dick. As she looked back up to his face she found him smirking down at her.

Damn, totally busted like some kind of hoochie for checking out a guy who wasn't her Master.

She was such a lousy submissive.

Something in Ivan's gaze sharpened, and she looked away, unable to hide from his scrutiny. He removed his jacket and held it out to her, revealing a crisp white shirt that stretched out over his impossibly broad shoulders. "Your Master wishes you to wear this so you don't get cold. Though your American fall is like the summer in Russia, that little scrap of nothing won't protect you from the chill."

Unsure if he wanted her to respond, she simply nodded and let him help her into the jacket. He looked down at her and gave her a small smile that made her heart lurch. With a gentle touch, he draped the heavy coat around her. It hung to almost her knees and held the scent of his cologne and natural musk. She pulled it tight and gave him a grateful smile.

"Thank you."

"What is your safeword?"

She blinked at him and tugged his jacket closer. "Damascus."

"Damascus? Like the city?"

"Yes, Sir." Both men looked at her, obviously expecting more of an answer so she babbled out, "My mother was part Syrian. We would visit there in the summer every other year when I was little."

The man nodded and took a step back, obviously putting some distance between them. She worried he thought she flirted with him. All she needed was her new Master thinking she was the kind of submissive who would screw anyone that smiled at her.

Ivan gave her another searching look before he turned. She followed, trying to at least walk gracefully. Mistress Viola had once said a submissive should be like a living work of art, graceful and flowing, a pleasure to the eye and touch, a joy to behold.

While she would probably never be anyone's joy to behold, at least she wouldn't embarrass her new Master. With the big strides Ivan was taking she wasn't as smooth as usual. Instead she clutched his jacket around herself and hurried after him. They passed a few other couples on their way through the mansion, including a Master who was rather vigorously fucking his new female submissive on the bottom steps of a set of stairs.

Lucky girl.

All too soon, they reached the front door. Ivan stopped and looked down at her bare feet. Standing this close to him made her feel small, feminine, and vulnerable. Without a word, he scooped her up into his arms as if she weighed nothing. She gave a somewhat undignified squeak and instinctively laced her arms around his neck. The sensation of his rock solid muscle surrounding her was arousing, and made her feel safe even as she scolded her body for responding to the wrong man. She looked up at him as he carried her outside and studied his profile. He had the look of some old time warlord, the kind of man who conquered the world in his spare time.

No, she needed to keep her focus on her new Master, whoever he was. Making herself look away, she studied the drive in front of the mansion and the cars parked there. Ivan headed to the left and tucked her closer to his body as a stiff wind filled with the spicy scent of fall leaves tickled her nose. He radiated warmth and she removed her hands from around his neck before tucking them against his chest.

They reached a black limo and a tall, lean man in a silver suit stood beside it. He had dark brown hair and grey eyes, and a well-trimmed beard. When he spotted her, he didn't say anything, merely nodded at Ivan and opened the door before getting into the limo.

She pushed at Ivan's chest. "Please let me go, I need to properly greet my Master."

Ivan looked down at the pavement then back at her feet. "No."

Befuddled, she found herself in the limo before she knew it with her new Master sitting at the front near the partition between the passenger section and the driver. She quickly took a seat at the long bench along the side of the limo, unsure if she should sit next to her new Master or wait for him to motion her over. He certainly didn't appear eager for her to join him. When she smiled and tried to catch his eyes, he looked away. Ivan climbed in after her and took the back seat between the two doors. As they pulled away from the mansion, she wished the week was already over.

For the rest of this story, check out Ann's website to find your local retailer

Did you enjoy this selection? Why not try another romance from Fated Desires?

Ever After

A Paranormal Anthology

From five bestselling authors comes five brand new novellas sure to heat up the night.

From **Carrie Ann Ryan**'s Dante's Circle series, a demon from the fiery depths of hell must make his choice to follow in the footsteps of his father or love the submissive wolf who lays claim to his heart in His Choice.

From **Marie Harte**'s Beasts of Burden, Eira, a fierce valkyrie, has spent fifty years trying to get a rise out of her goddess's guardians. But when the battle-cat shifters give her what she wants, can she handle the heat—and the danger—that comes from loving them?

From **Rebecca Royce**'s brand new series, the Alphas of each Werewolf Pack are on the brink of war. Travis Michaels will use all in his power to keep innocent Lilliana out of danger and into his arms...away from rival Alpha Cyrus Fennell.

From **Lia Davis**'s Ashwood Falls series, buried pain, old lies, and dangerous secrets aren't enough to keep the sparks from flying as Sarah Mathews and rebel leader, Damian Archer, try to survive a new threat against their race.

From **Leia Shaw**'s Shadows of Destiny series, a war is brewing in the supernatural world. Rebel shifter Dalton's only passion is protecting the colony, and flirtatious misfit, Eden, is a distraction he can't afford. But as danger approaches, he learns that underestimating the sexy little wolf is a big mistake.

Did you enjoy this selection? Why not try another romance from Fated Desires?

From Rebecca Royce's The Capes Series

Seductive Powers

This title has been previously published and has been re-edited for your enjoyment.

Wendy Warner is a bit of an oddball. Raised in an orphanage, she's found solace and friendship by watching the television show, *Space Adventures*, and participating in its fan clubs. Twice a month, Wendy comes to work dressed in a costume from the show that she wears to charity events. She's been able to ignore the looks of distain from many of her coworkers, but when the president of the company gazes at her with something more, she knows she's in deep.

Draco Powers rather likes the way the uniform hugs all her curves in the just the right places. He's also a real-life Guardian who told the world that, yes, some people had superhuman abilities, but, no, they wouldn't work for free or without health insurance. Some people refer to him with derision as the

"Capitalist Guardian." While Draco doesn't care what he's called, he's also being hunted by a group called the Organization, whose motives are unclear and yet still cause death and destruction wherever they go.

The Organization has decided that Draco's biggest weakness is the way he cares about his employees and has chosen Wendy as their next target. To save her, Draco will have to come to terms with his real feelings and the reason he's long resisted complicated relationships...but he's running out of time.